JENNA DIETZER

Fear Her

The Lovebugs originally published by New Gothic Review

End of Day originally published in Jolly Horror Press's Executive Dread Anthology

Those Who Wish to be Clean originally published by Coffin Bell Journal

Daughters originally published in Scare Street Night Terrors Vol. 21

First edition

Cover art by Tea Jagodic
Editing by Patricia McCarthy, Seeing Eye Editing

This book was professionally typeset on Reedsy.
Find out more at reedsy.com

For Her

And for Imogene,
who always woke me
to watch Tales from the Crypt

Contents

Foreword

By: Wendy Dalrymple

What is it that you fear? Bugs? Sharp objects? Shadowy figures? Strange men? This collection of short stories from my fellow Florida Gothic author Jenna Dietzer uncovers all of the dark places of the feminine experience and touches on fears that everyone can relate to. *Fear Her* explores the notion of what it means to live in this world as a woman and all of the icky, sticky aspects of being feminine. But you don't have to be female to understand and identify with the blood-soaked themes that run through this collection. From self-harm, psychological fears, human monsters and more, Dietzer offers readers perfectly packaged, bite-sized tales of terror.

I first met Jenna over a decade ago when we were working together as copywriters. Neither of us knew it at the time, but we were both secretly horror loving junkies and aspiring fiction writers. I knew she and I were meant to be friends when she wrote a two-sentence horror story during a corporate creative writing workshop that absolutely blew me away. That story still lives rent-free in my mind every time I look out a window late at night. Jenna continues to be one of my greatest supporters, friends and reading buddies and I am so proud to see her first collection of works be shared with you all.

So grab a cup of coffee and settle into this macabre anthology of female-driven horrors, and remember, there's nothing to fear but fear herself.

Content Warnings

These stories may contain depictions of miscarriage, self-harm (cutting), disordered eating, kidnapping, death of a partner, death of a pet, mental illness, body horror, and/or suicide.

Drawing Flies

You tell the therapist "I don't . . . *hate* my body." But she's not convinced.

It's that long pause you took before the word 'hate,' the way your voice lifted at the end of your sentence, like a question instead of a fact.

She traipses through a garden of inspirations, from "girl power" to "your body is a temple." Blah blah blah. Those flowers are all pretty, you want to tell her, but they have no perfume.

You stare as she continues to jabber, wondering why she was your previous therapist's referral, wondering why your previous therapist said both that they needed to take a break for personal reasons and that they were worried about you. Maybe this was the only other therapist available.

She jots down some notes and grows quiet. It's not the first thing that bothers you but the second.

Shit. You pinch the skin of your wrist.

"Tell me about those," she says, pointing to your arms with her pen.

You glance down. The outer wrist, the side she can see, is pockmarked with scabs, some deep and some shallow. You could tell her they're mosquito bites because it's summer, and you couldn't resist the itch even though you knew it would make you bleed.

But she knows that's not why you're here.

"Can I see?" She mimes with her hands what she wants you to do with your own, revealing her soft, unblemished inner wrists. Her delicate fingers curl toward them.

You don't want to show her, but you do, but only for a second. *Don't be difficult*, you coach yourself. It's just long enough for her to see the pale hash marks drawn across your skin. They resemble little ladder rungs climbing toward your elbows. There are some larger welts, too, from that time you borrowed a cigarette and let it burn and burn. The scars pucker like shiny, curled worms. They squish under your touch.

She asks "Why?" and that's when you know she really is bad at this therapist thing, like a lover who rushes through foreplay. She startles you. It should have taken at least two or three sessions to get there. Where are the questions about your parents' divorce, your fucked up ex? The mood is ruined.

You hug one of the couch pillows and reply, "Why not?"

You mean it innocently, but she takes it as sarcasm. This displeases her, and the corners of her lips turn down. You're an idiot, you remind yourself. They're going to send you back for treatment—a longer, hospital-mandated visit again—if you keep this up.

You flash back to the hospital and your mom's face, the same downturned lips when she saw your exposed arms and legs and back. A human cutting board. Her eyes welled, and her right hand stifled a gasp. For a while, you felt guilty for being a burden to her; to everyone. But that was erased when she asked you, in all seriousness, which social media trend had put this thought into your head. You laughed like a mad woman until she picked up her purse and left. She barely answers your calls now, always going to voicemail. It's better this way.

The therapist is still frowning, waiting for you to answer her sincerely. Your eyes flit to the clock, and you both realize there are only five minutes left.

You don't tell her about the razor blade buried in the purse beside you. You don't tell her how you'll drive home and park after this session. Then you'll remove the razor blade from its pouch pocket and dig somewhere fresh, until the pain is worse than the last time. It must feel worse than the last time, or what's the point? Or you may even reopen a wound that's already healed.

You don't tell her how this makes you happy—happier than anything else, because the torture is magic. It gives you a buzz more intense than your own rage, sorrow, or emptiness. And the blood, the seeping tender wounds purge your thoughts and leave you more relaxed than any drug ever could. It helps you sleep. Sleep with deep, intoxicating dreams.

Instead you clear your throat and dance through a conversation about her availability next week, knowing the appointment is a sham. You won't return. This isn't a good fit. You'll have to start from scratch all over again.

It's late and dark by the time you reach your car. While driving home, you rummage for that razor blade as the thoughts intensify. *You're such a weirdo. You'll never get better. Why do you have to make such a big deal out of everything?* And when you can't find the blade, you raise your wrist to your mouth and bite it hard. You imagine you're a wild dog, attacking, ready to tear off the limb. It doesn't bleed, but your teeth dig in so deep you feel the blood vessels burst below the flesh. When you let go, you see your arm in the passing streetlights. The spot is swollen and protruding between the bite marks, already bruising.

Good, you think. You hope it hurts all week. You hope it serves as a reminder.

Then you hear a thud beneath your tires, the shriek of an animal. Your car jumps and swerves as you catch the steering wheel. In the rearview mirror, a figure flies off the road and into a field of cornstalks. It disappears into the shadows as you continue to drive.

Fuck. The word balloons in your head, threatening to swallow your other thoughts. It swells and swells, until you're screaming at yourself and banging your bruised arm against the dash.

Inside the house you take another razor blade from the bathroom drawer and, with one quick slash, cut along your cheekbone. The droplets of blood stream from the laceration like tears. They trickle down to your chin and onto your shirt. You don't wipe them away. As they slow and clot, you feel some relief.

The next morning, you wash and dress the wound along your cheekbone. It's still tender to the touch. Still alive, still healing. Your appetite is nil, but your brain is chewing again: *You're a fuck-up. Who would do that to a poor creature? You must go back.*

You call work and tell them you won't be in for your shift again today. They're no longer surprised. They no longer ask questions and, to be honest, you're not sure you still have a job.

You park at a stop sign about one hundred yards from where you hit the thing last night. It's foggy this morning, but your tire skids and a dark trail of blood materialize along the road as you walk toward the spot. There's a buzz, not from an approaching car engine, but up ahead. You pull your hands against your chest only to find they're shivering. You pinch the firm outer skin of your new bruise between your nails to quiet your hands.

The row of cornstalks sways toward you and the road, momentarily blocking your view. When they stop, you see the limp, furry body and the source of the buzzing.

Flies. Hundreds of them swarming around the corpse. They look as if they could reanimate it. You creep closer and squat beside the carcass. It reeks of decay. You hide your mouth and nose from the stench with your hand.

The flies' unblinking, blood-moon eyes and mechanic movements and polished, iridescent bodies remind you of robots. They crawl erratically across the peeled-back flesh of the abdomen, the agape mouth leaking with blood. Or maybe it's that they crawl ecstatically, like toddlers drunk on sugar. You wonder what their bodies do with the pieces they consume.

Between the flies and the maggots, one of the hind quarters of the animal is already peeling away from the torso. Its eyes are lifeless, staring off into the cornfield, and the fur is matted with dry, stiff blood. A silver tag dangles from a black collar at its throat.

You fan away the flies and grasp the tag between your fingers and read the name "Teddy" then a home address and telephone number.

Your heart sinks into your bowels. You are a pet-murdering, hit-and-run, goddamn piece of shit. You pick at the scab on your cheek until it stings. When you draw back your hand, your fingertips are wet with blood. You stare at it for a moment. Then you pick yourself up and walk back to your car and turn on the ignition. You repeat the address in your brain at every stop sign until you find a house that matches the road and house number.

You wait. You clean the blood from your cheek with spit and a napkin from your glove compartment. The blinds of the house are drawn, and there are no cars in the driveway. The house looks tattered, poor, with peeled paint and leaking gutters. If it were a person, it would be sad. Something about it is familiar to you.

Maybe this was for the best, you think. Maybe they let the dog run wild because they couldn't take care of it.

Then a voice calls out "Can I help you?" from beside the house.

It's a young woman, perhaps high school age. She's skinny but not malnourished. Her hair is in braids. She squints against the sun and keeps her distance from your idle car. She knows not to trust strangers.

The words practically vomit from your mouth. "Te-teddy? Are you Teddy's mom? Do you have a dog named Teddy?"

Calm down, you idiot. You're going to scare the shit out of her.

She nods her head yes slowly, skeptically, until the realization lights up her face. "Where?" she asks, and you offer to drive her there. To your surprise, she doesn't say no. During the drive, she is quiet. She picks at her fingernails and pulls at her eyelashes.

The silence is maddening, and every part of you wants to peel back the cut along your cheek, until the muscle and bones are exposed, until you can fold the loose skin up over your eyes and hide from what's about to happen.

You park in the same spot where you parked before. Walk the same direction you previously went. She follows until you're both standing beside the dead dog.

A lump forms in your throat and you're about to say something, anything to interrupt this moment. Then a low hum emits from her open mouth. It sounds like the buzzing of the flies at first, that deep, persistent hum. Then it grows louder and stronger, rapidly, and blossoms into a scream. She screams at the dog carcass for what feels like several minutes before losing her breath. She gasps for air and clutches her hand to yours, the nails digging into your flesh.

Another scream tears from her lips, and this time you join her. She only lets go of your hand once your throats have gone hoarse, brows beaded with sweat and cheeks flushed. The scab on your cheek breaks and weeps again, but this time you don't wipe away the blood.

She doesn't want what remains of Teddy, not even the collar. She just wanted to see it. She leaves it to the flies, their thrum fizzling out as you walk back to your car.

You drive her home. In the driveway, she asks what happened to your cheek, pointing to the seeping scab, then what happened to your arm. She fixates on your scars just like your new therapist, all the nurses; like your mother. Yet the corners of her lips do not frown. You don't know what to say.

You want to confess. You want to tell her you're sorry. You want to take it all back. Not telling her feels like the second time you've hurt this stranger in less than 24 hours. But more than anything, you want to sink your teeth into your arm and burst open that throbbing bruise. She exits your vehicle and doesn't turn to wave goodbye.

You're surprised to find yourself sitting in the new therapist's office the next afternoon, talking about the corpse, the scream-ing teenager, the flies. She doesn't bring up the cut along your cheek, which you appreciate. But you leave out the part about biting yourself because you don't trust her with it yet.

This feels good, you think. Talking about it. The relief isn't as deep as cutting, but it's a start. Maybe you won't deface your limbs tonight, but you make yourself no promises. The hematoma on your forearm, hidden by the long, puffy sleeves you purposefully chose, has swollen to the size of a golf ball. It's moist and discolored around the sores your bite marks left. Your fingers feel stiff under its weight.

Before the therapist has a chance to ask any questions, you tell her more about the flies. How flies taste with their feet. How they can smell death within 15 minutes of it happening. How they lay their eggs in feces and rotting corpses so their hatched larva can feed.

The therapist raises a hand to stop you.

"Tell me how you felt in that moment," she instructs.

She and you both know that is impossible.

"Sad? Mad? Frightened?" she prompts.

Impossible.

"Because you've spent twenty minutes talking about the flies and none talking about you."

That's wrong, you think. You've been talking about you and the flies this whole time, with their bristled legs like serrated knife edges. You pause for a moment, grasping for words that might make sense.

"I want to be . . . the dog," you finally say.

You watch as her mouth twists in uncertainty. Then her eyes widen. "Yes! Good. Okay. So you wish you could switch places with the dog. Guilt can make us feel that way. Right? Let's work through that together."

She asks you to close your eyes and breathe deeply three times with her, which you don't refuse. This train of thought is already too far down the tracks. She walks you through an exercise where you focus on each part of your body, breathing into it and relaxing it. It doesn't work. Your previous therapist would never ask you to do this. You feel uncomfortable again. You want to be numb.

Halfway through, as she's guiding you through relaxing your arms, you open your eyes. Her eyes are, indeed, closed. She's all in, and she's getting more out of this than you are. Your mind drifts to memories of the flies, crawling, feeding on flesh. You imagine them landing on her closed eyes, consuming her face, consuming your own. Your breath accelerates, and you pick at the hot skin beneath your shirt. You dig your fingernails against the bulged bruise, until the pain overtakes your wrist, knuckle, and elbow, until you feel anesthetized.

When it's done you both open your eyes to flushed cheeks and mirrored smiles.

"Better?" she asks.

You nod your head. "Better."

She hands you a worksheet and asks you to complete it before your next session. *Happy-work, not homework*, she calls it. The title is something about repressed emotions. You wonder if the edges of the worksheet would make deep paper cuts.

On the way back home you pull off to the side of the road again, where the flies and maggots, their feeding babies, are congregated and growing. Vultures have picked over the carcass, and all that's left of the hind quarter from yesterday is a bit of muscle and bone.

Warm sun pours in like honey on the flies. The air feels hot, like the sunset is burning down the earth. You wipe your brow. One of the flies drifts closer to your sleeve, circling your arm. You don't swat it away. You let it land on the soft, ballooning fabric and watch its mechanical legs inch down to your wrist. Your hand is visibly swollen now. The skin appears sunburnt, one of the fingernails darkening. Your fingers barely tingle with circulation.

You draw up the sleeve to find the bruise is blistered and sweating, the edges a morbid red. The fly on your sleeve is intrigued. It plods onto the gooey surface and begins to feed. It feels like a tickle against the tender, exposed nerve endings that remain. You ache and moan, and your breath flutters through your lungs. Then it ignites into a whole new feeling you can't describe. It's the closest you've ever felt to crawling out of your skin.

You drop to one knee and dig through your purse. You turn it inside out. Then a shining slip of metal falls into the grass. You take the razor blade into your hand and peel back the infected flesh, offering it to the flies. They dance on the open, cascading wound.

Breathless and dizzy, you crawl into the corn field, away from the road. The flies follow, and you let them swarm and sink into the gash. They cover your eyes. You breathe them in. You taste them in your mouth. You feel no thirst or hunger now. You are full of a single feeling. *Pain.* Its delicious, unrelenting warmth crowds into your skull and limbs, pushing out everything else. Just like the maggots. Just like you'd hoped it would be.

In a few days, the young woman, the one with braids in her hair, walks past your hidden corpse on her way to the store. She smells you first and mistakes it for the smell of Teddy but then notices the flies circling between the tall stalks of corn. She veers and wanders into the field and sees your dissolving body. What remains of your face is drawn into a smile. Your exposed arm still wields its staircase of puckered tissue. The nicks on your hands are a constellation of stars.

Her mouth is taut as she examines you. No sadness or judgment show on her face. She observes the razor blade beside your body and picks it up. There are traces of dark fluid along its blade. But even as she wipes it along her pant leg, it doesn't budge. She cradles your razor in her hands and backs out of the cornfield, leaving your rotted body to rest among the tire skids, the brutal sun, the endless buzzing. Without a flinch, she draws the blade across her arm, just enough to pierce the skin.

X

My first weeks as a Florida transplant and college freshman almost crushed me. Surrounded by strangers and dizzying heat, all I wanted to do was hide. And since a dorm room with paper-thin walls wasn't much of a home, I hid myself in the library. Inside it was cool and barely lit and quiet except for rustling. It was also where Yara found me.

I was walking toward another afternoon of feeling sorry for myself when Yara stepped between me and the library steps. She wore our school colors, crimson and brown, and a cascade of blonde hair poured over her shoulders. She offered a smile and slipped a flier into my hands.

"You should come," she said.

I looked down at the paper. In the center was a large, dark 'X' and, in smaller font below it, an address on the outskirts of campus.

"What is this?" I asked.

She stepped around to my left and pressed her shoulder against mine. In her hair, I could smell traces of coconut. Her smile was a perfect bow of pink.

"We're a sorority," she said pointing at the flier. "The X is the Greek letter Chi, and that's the address of our sorority house.

Rush starts next week, and you look like someone who'd fit in at Chi house."

I eyed the flier then Yara skeptically. She had a celebrity tan, pouty lips, and nothing short of perfect skin. Classic Florida girl. If every other member of Chi was as pretty as her, then I would clearly not fit in. My northeastern skin burned too easily here.

"What makes you think I'd fit in?" I asked.

"Well, you're headed toward the library, which means you're smart. So are we. You look like you could use some support. That's what we're all about."

The words sounded tempting, but if I was reading between the lines, she'd called out my strangeness as an obvious bullseye.

Yara noted my silence. "What's your name?"

"Rachel."

"It's nice to meet you, Rachel. My name is Yara." She wrapped an arm around me, half-hugging, as if she were consoling an old friend. "I felt lonely and out of place just like you during my first weeks here. Chi can help. That's what they did for me. That's the power of a sorority."

She sashayed off, taking her sweet aroma with her, and disappeared into the crowd of students.

No one else approached me about joining their sorority that week. No one even seemed to notice me. I beetled from the dorm to the library to the cafeteria as if I were a ghost. So on Friday night, as I looked across an empty library and munched on my vending machine candy bar, I summoned the confidence to walk to Chi house. Maybe this could turn my fate around, as it had for Yara.

The sorority house had a face of pale-yellow bricks. Black shutters framed rows of large windows poised above the sloping lawn. Mint green tiles covered the roof. In the center of the house were two white columns supporting an awning where the letter 'X' was painted. Scattered across the Chi lawn were seven or eight other hopefuls—fewer than I'd expected.

At 10 p.m., several of the sisters emerged from the house. Yara waved when she spotted me but didn't move from her station in the lineup of girls. One of them called for us to approach the steps. Another passed out slips of paper and pens. She told us to write our names at the tops of our papers and then to write down our answers to the question.

What are your top 3 fears? was the question at the top of my paper.

I glanced around at the other rushes, who were already pressing their squares of paper against purses, each other's backs, and the backs of their own hands to spill their confessions.

I thought for a moment then wrote:

1) Death

2) Losing my mind

3) Cockroaches

When everyone on the lawn handed back their papers, the sisters told us to return the following Friday, when a decision would be made. Then they marched back into the house and shut the door.

Those of us left glanced around at each other and huddled along the sidewalk.

"What the hell was that?" one of us asked.

"Yeah. No parties. No events. Nothing about getting matched," explained another. "It sounds like they're going to judge us based on our fears alone, which is a dick move."

We nodded our heads in collective agreement.

"Actually, I think I know what's going to happen," a third

chimed in. We all turned toward her, and she lowered her voice. "My older sister told me about Chi. She's a school alum. This sorority's mantra is 'fearless females.' So isn't it obvious?" My face wasn't the only one that went blank. She gave us all an exasperated sigh. "They're going to make us confront our fears in order to get in."

I swallowed hard as I remembered what I wrote. They couldn't kill me or make me crazy. But the cockroaches, that was possible. Florida was littered with them, especially in the September heat. We even had an entomology department, where a lot of dudes studied bugs. It just took knowing the right person.

"Are you sure?" I whispered.

She nodded. "I'd bet on it."

We stood in a silent circle, filled with anxiety, until the girl next to me started walking off. "There's no way I'm letting one of these bitches draw my blood or put me in a room with a clown," she called over her shoulder. "There are plenty of other sororities. Peace out, Chi. You can take rush week and shove it."

One by one, the other pledges walked off, until three of us remained.

The girl whose sister knew about Chi's reputation turned to me. "What did you write down?"

"Roaches," I confessed. "I hate roaches. One fell in my mouth when I was a kid."

She cringed. "That sounds pretty awful. But it also sounds like there's nothing they can do to you that's worse than that." I considered this and nodded in agreement. "One of mine was public speaking," she confessed. "If I'm being honest, facing that fear would help me more than it would harm me."

"And what were your other two?"

"Death and heights. Obviously, they can't do much about the first one. But I'm scared enough of heights that I might not come back either. They'd probably want me to bungee jump or something ridiculous like that." She shuddered.

Eventually we disbanded, but my mind was plagued by the strange ceremony on the lawn for the rest of the next week. I thought about roaches each time I sat in the musty, silent library, flinched at every creeping shadow on my dorm room floor, and had nightmares of roaches crawling into my open mouth as I slept. My rational brain told me there was no way they'd haze us with our fears. Greek hazing alone had gotten enough bad press for them to think twice.

Still, with the end of rush week looming and no other chance to speak to Chi before it ended, there seemed little else we could do to win their favor. What I'd written on that piece of paper was more significant than I cared to admit.

I looked for Yara on the library lawn again and thought how brave she was to approach complete strangers with a flier, to move in with women she didn't know, to overcome fear. Every sister who stood in front of the pledges that night was just as confident. Effortlessly. It was as if they held the secret to not only surviving but thriving at college.

So I found myself beneath Chi house's large X the following Friday. I'd purchased a special dress for the event—floral and innocent looking. Part of me hoped the fear tests would be a mistake, that we'd do sister speed dating instead and pop a bottle of champagne at the end. In my nervousness, I kept tugging at the hem of my dress.

I was the only one at the door. I checked my watch. 10 p.m. on the nose. Yet all the lights were off inside, like a house without candy on Halloween. I wondered if 'd misheard the start time or if none of the other pledges were coming back after all. I pressed a finger against Chi's doorbell and waited as the sound echoed.

Then giggling bubbled up deep within the house.

"Hello?" I shouted.

The door swung back to reveal candlelight flickering against the ceiling and corridor. Perhaps one of the pledges had written that she was afraid of the dark.

The sister in the foyer directed me to the left, toward what looked like a living room. The rest of the sisters stood with their backs pressed against the walls. Although faces were hard to discern in the shadows, I didn't see any of the other pledges among them. Yara stood in the center with a wooden box in her hands and an empty chair in front of her—the only piece of furniture in the room.

"Here, Rach. May I call you Rach?"

She beckoned me with her hand and that familiar warm smile.

"Have a seat."

I hesitated.

The girl behind me gently pushed me forward, saying, "Now, now. You came back because you wanted to be a part of Chi. It's just a chair."

I gulped, and as I walked toward the chair, my breath caught in my lungs. The other pledge was right, I told myself. They couldn't do anything worse to me than that first experience of the cockroach wiggling inside my mouth. If I could make it through the next half hour, I could make it through anything.

I sat down, and Yara sank to one knee beside me. Our eyes met.

"Rachel, last Friday you shared with us that your fears were death, losing your mind, and cockroaches."

I felt naked.

"The answer to overcoming those fears is Chi," she said. "Will you say it with us?" She paused. "Chi," and then again, "Chi."

"Chi," I whispered. My voice felt hidden in my throat.

She repeated it back to me, raising her own voice, until mine grew louder.

"Chi."

The word pricked on every sister's tongue, spreading across the room. "Chi. Chi. Chi."

Yara pulled back the wooden box's lid to reveal a dead cockroach inside. Six spindly legs curled against its caramel belly. Two antennae formed a V above its small head.

The sisters hushed.

I winced as she pinched the antennae between her manicured fingertips and dangled it in front of my face.

"Eat it," Yara said. "Own your fear. Let it become part of you."

I turned my cheek and recoiled at the memory of the cockroach that had accidentally passed my lips when I was a child. My tongue desperately pushing it out. The brush of its flimsy shell along my teeth. The wiggling of its legs against my gums and lips as it crawled out.

"Chi," the room whispered in unison. "Chi. Chi," they insisted.

This one's dead, I consoled myself. Not like the other. Just swallow. Swallow and it will all be over.

I closed my eyes and leaned back my head. My mouth yawned wide. I could feel Yara's hand move, to dangle the roach above me. When it landed, it was already deep inside my mouth. But it was thick, like swallowing a giant pill. The limbs and thorax scraped along my throat, so I swallowed and swallowed again. Beads of sweat trickled from my temples, and I thought I might vomit.

But I didn't. Eventually the tightness in my throat released.

I opened my eyes as the candles extinguished and lamplight came on. The sisters swarmed around me with their hands clasped and elbows touching. Approving smiles swept across their faces.

"Damn, girl," Yara said. "You did it. Now you're a member of Chi!"

Balloons, filled with confetti, popped and showered over us. A beer appeared in my hand. The sisters introduced themselves and congratulated me while music pulsed throughout the house. This was the celebration I'd wanted. I'd finally found my place. We danced, we smoked, we chatted. And I drank and drank, until I was sure I'd washed down every trace of that roach, until my head spun with each step and lights and faces doubled before me.

Later, Yara watched as I sat alone on that chair in the middle of the room, staring at the floor and babbling to the fallen confetti pieces.

She grabbed my shoulders and shook me softly. "Why don't you just stay here tonight, Rach? You'll be moving into Chi house soon anyway. We have an agreement with the dorms. If you make it, you come live with us." She patted my back. "It's like you're already home."

"Home," I breathed. The thank-yous slipped from my tongue again and again as she guided me up the stairs.

"Goodnight, *Roach*," one of the sorority sisters teased as we climbed to the second story.

"Shh," Yara hissed down the stairs. Then she turned back to me. "Don't mind Becky. She's just bitter because this is her last year at Chi house. Next year she has to be a fucking adult."

"Adult?" I made a raspberry noise to that, and we laughed all the way up.

That night, in my hazy drunkenness, I dreamed the dead cockroach squirmed out of my throat and nested on my lips until morning.

* * *

After initiation, my life didn't improve much. Most of the time, even Saturday morning after our party, I woke to an empty Chi house. No one roomed with me because, according to Yara, they were still trying to find a good fit after "the cockroach thing."

Whenever I returned from class, the rooms were abandoned and strangely quiet, as if I'd stumbled into a haunted house. The only sign of life were little notes taped to the refrigerator or the door to my room.

Out to lunch! Wish you could've come, Rachel! X

or just *We'll be back soon, Rach!* X

The exclamation points only made it worse. Those fake, stabbing cuts. Their message—addressed only to me—were a reminder that I was the only one being left out.

They also left me food. A ham or peanut butter sandwich, pizza slices, lukewarm soup, a bowl of cereal. Like a child coming home after school to an empty house and absent parents, I devoured each plate. Sometimes I was hungry. Sometimes I just wanted to comfort myself.

I didn't blame them. Each time they saw me, they probably saw that dangling, lifeless cockroach and my jaw ready for it. I felt disgusting.

In mid-October, I found a probationary letter on my door instead of a note. The letter listed out the days and times of meetings I'd missed and warned that if I missed two more, my Chi membership would be suspended. Apparently our house meetings were held every other week at midnight—while I was asleep.

Yara slipped past my room while I read the note.

"Hey, when is our next house meeting?" I called after her. "I seemed to have missed a few. I didn't even know we had them."

I handed Yara the letter. She seemed frazzled and irritated at first. But as she read, her face softened. "Someone must've sent this to you by mistake. New members aren't obligated to attend their first semester." She handed the letter back to me and offered a reassuring smile.

"Anyway, we've decided to pause the meetings for now. I'll let someone know they made a mistake. Don't worry."

Before I could thank her, she'd scurried back down the stairs. I didn't even hear the front door shut.

I assumed she was telling me the truth until, one week later, I woke in the middle of the night to rustling noises downstairs. When I followed the sounds I found them. All of them, huddled in the kitchen. They swarmed around a few candles and an island filled with party snacks. Cubes of cheese, sliced meats, chips and crackers.

When they spotted me in the doorway they hushed. Yara gulped when our eyes met, and I realized this must be one of the infamous house meetings, which had clearly not been 'paused.'

My cheeks grew hot.

"Rach! So glad you could make it to one of our meetings!" Yara said, recovering quickly. "Of course, you weren't obligated." She rose from her chair. "Here. Sit. We were just about to discuss our plans for Halloween."

A hole formed in the center of the sisters, just as it had on initiation night. My skin clammed up at the memory. In the middle of the table sat a shallow bowl with folded pieces of paper.

"Pick one," Yara insisted, pushing the bowl toward me. She held up her own piece of paper between her fingertips.

"Why?" I asked.

"We've all decided to dress up as butterflies for Halloween. Tutus, wings, tights, leotards." The sisters nodded their heads. "And we were picking our colors by seniority. Everyone's gone but you. Perfect timing."

"We're picking butterfly colors?" I clarified.

She nodded. "Yeah. One color per sister. This Friday we'll take the trolley to Ybor for a Halloween pub crawl. Fluttering and wasted. It'll be fun."

I stared at the bowl, hesitating.

Across from me, Becky let out a sigh. "Jesus, Rachel. It's not a bowl of bugs. Just pick a color."

Yara swatted at her.

My fingers swam through the paper pieces until I caught the edge of one. I lifted it, unfolded it, and read it aloud with disappointment tinging my voice: "Brown."

"Gross." Becky said. "Just like you, *Roach*."

Becky was pummeled with moans and protests from the rest of the sisters.

I glared at her, but in a way, she was right. How was I supposed to find brown butterfly wings? Was that even a thing? And how was I supposed to make it into an attractive costume by Friday? I was destined to feel disgusting in front of them once again.

"You could always do copper, Rach," Yara offered. "Like, really sparkly. It'll be pretty!"

I frowned at her. "What color are you?"

"White, of course." She beamed perfect teeth at me.

We all munched and made small talk, took pulls from a shared bottle of tequila Becky snuck in, and chased it with several rounds of beers.

Just as I was feeling warm and fuzzy, Beck shouted, "Meeting adjourned! Time for bed!" and the sisters scattered from sight.

In the morning, my head ached from a hangover, and my jaw was clenched and tight. There was a puffy, numb feeling about my face when I touched it. I wondered if I'd dreamt the whole thing or if I had a drinking problem when a crumbled slip of paper with the word "brown" fell from my hand. Friday was just around the corner.

* * *

The trolley ride into Ybor on Halloween was too chilly for our costumes. High top sneakers, bikini tops, tutus, necklaces, and wings. Every other sister looked dazzling and buzzing with life, while I, in my matte brown fabric, resembled a moth.

"You look great, Rach," Yara whispered as the car rattled along the track. I knew she was lying, but I appreciated her trying to make me feel better. White sparkles clung to her high cheekbones and shimmered underneath each streetlight we passed. The tips of her wings swayed with the streetcar in a way that made me giggle.

Becky turned around in her seat. "Roach cleans up pretty good when she's not busy eating bugs."

Yara frowned. "Shut up, Becky. It's not like you should be proud of what got you in either."

Becky's face reddened for a moment, then she glared at us through foggy, cheap-liquor eyes. My stomach twisted, but not just because I expected Becky to slug me at some point tonight. I'd also downed a ton of alcohol at the house, just like her. Just like all the sisters. Our plan was to arrive wasted, then nurse just one or two of the expensive club drinks until it was time to go home.

Gradually, the sharp edges of the evening dulled. The booming basses softened, the glowing lights became hazy, and the clanging glasses at the bar sounded a million miles away.

The last thing I remember was worming into a narrow alleyway to vomit. The concrete bit into my kneecaps and palms as I bent on all fours to retch. Then wet wisps of hair beside my mouth were pulled back and away gently. A hand rested on my shoulder. It reminded me of Yara's hand from that first day outside of the library. A cloth pressed against my nose and lips. Then the hand smothered my face.

* * *

I woke up in darkness. No windows. No light filling the edges of the room. Had it been my own room at the sorority house, I could have seen outlines in the moonlight. Door handles, picture frame edges, my own bedspread. But this place was a void. A black sink with black water. Everywhere my limbs swam, I grasped onto nothing.

I stayed where I woke for a long time, afraid to move anymore. Hours passed. Maybe days. I couldn't tell. Sticky hot sweat dripped from my face and armpits and never seemed to evaporate.

Was I in a coma at the hospital? Had I been swallowed by some creature? Was this death?

Then the tiniest sliver of light escaped through the base of the wall against my back. It illuminated enough for me to see I wasn't inside of a creature, but a room with a wooden floor and no escape. A low, vaulted ceiling with exposed wooden beams hung above me like a rib cage. Everything smelled of must and sweat and piss. Was it my piss?

My hands slid along the floor, through dust piles and gravel, until a small square materialized in the middle of the room. The smell of peanut butter hit my nostrils, and I leapt toward it, until my hands felt the softness of sandwich bread.

My stomach grumbled as I shoved it into my mouth. The peanut butter crunched and squished between my teeth. My brain begged me to slow down, to make sure I wouldn't vomit. But I resisted. Chunks fell like rocks into the cavern of my stomach until the sandwich was gone.

Some time passed while I glanced around the room, wondering how the sandwich got in here and why I'd been brought here myself. I couldn't tell if I'd been beaten or tortured, because the crack in the wall barely offered enough light to reveal the floorboards and ceiling, let alone my own body.

Every part of me ached. I knew that much. I rolled over to my side to peel off my clothes but lost the energy as soon as my hands reached my feet. I stayed there on the floorboard, resting my head and staring into the crack of the wall . My will to stay awake faded with the light.

Just before I lost consciousness, I spotted a small creature creeping along the floor.

* * *

The second time I woke, the cleft of light was gone. I stretched out my arms and legs to see if I could find the wall again, but there was nothing. No food smells. No distinguishable sounds except my own languished breathing. I asked myself again if I had died or was somehow between death and whatever happened next. This caused my heart to kick in my chest, a solemn confirmation that, no, I was still captive and very much alive.

Suddenly, I heard a soft creak to my left, and pale-yellow light spilled onto the ceiling. My head turned, but by the time my eyes adjusted, all I could see was a hatch door and another plate in the center of the room.

"No," I whispered as I clambered toward the opening. "No."

It shut before I could reach it, so I banged at the patch of wooden planks with my fists. My voice was a phantom, scratchy and barely audible.

I sank into pity until my finger rediscovered the plate beside me. I lifted the sandwich to my nose. Ham and cheese with either mustard or mayo. Or both. My mouth salivated. How many hours had I been asleep this time? How long had I gone without food?

Then something stirred. I thought the floor was about to unlatch again, but when I focused harder, I realized the sound came from above.

Pat. Pat-pat. Pat-pat-pat. That was familiar. I remembered that noise. Pat-pat. The hard, full echo of raindrops beating against the roof. Pat.

My mind connected the pieces in rapid succession: the darkness, the overwhelming heat, the floorboards and beams above me, a door in the floor instead of a wall. I was in an attic.

My mind drifted, and I put down the sandwich plate. If the crack in the wall was the only place where light appeared—then disappeared—then it must be daylight. But how many hours away from reappearing? Would I be able to stay awake this time?

If the rain stopped and morning came, I could have hours of daylight to examine the dim room and plot my escape. Why hadn't I put this together before?

The sandwich was the only thing I could cling to, so I held on, refusing to eat it. I sat there for hours, meditating on every edge of the plate and sandwich, trying to hear the house below me breathe. The silence was deafening, and I wondered if the attic was in an abandoned house. Then the rain stopped. Sunshine trickled in slowly through the slot. Pink at first, then yellow. My eyes adjusted. I hadn't fallen asleep. In its small beam, dust muddied the view, but it was still enough for me to make out the shape of the attic again. I slid toward the cracked wall. The way the fabric peeled back gave me an idea.

I let go of the plate and sunk my fingernails into the edges of the gap and pulled. Hard. Some of the delicate layers fell away, revealing more light. I clawed and tugged, until it refused to budge.

A squirrel-sized hole now framed a world below me, although the view wasn't much. Just green at first, like a lawn. That wasn't surprising. My eye darted side to side and down further, trying to make out more than color. But it was no use. Something just below this wall blocked my view.

"Fuck," I whispered.

Then I heard laughter bubble up from inside the house. I pressed my ear against the floorboards as it grew closer. Where had I heard those voices before? Where had I—?

The sandwich sat in front of me, covered in dust. I felt my hands shaking as I reached for the top layer of bread and pulled it back.

Squished between the bread and ham slice was a thick, reddish-brown sludge. A wet, dead roach, with six spindly legs curled against its body.

"It can't be," I heard my hoarse voice whisper. Then I remembered the crunch of the peanut butter sandwich earlier.

I dropped the plate and its pieces scattered across the floor. I vomited until there was nothing left but dry heaves. Then the giggles below me turned to chants. "Chi ... Chi ... Chi."

My mind flashed to my first night at Chi house. The dizzy buzz of what I'd assumed was just fear and liquor. The roach. I ate a roach that night. All those times I arrived at an abandoned home with a sandwich waiting for me. I never looked inside, never assumed, never suspected. Even the night I woke to find them at their house meeting. Sandwiches waiting for me. A bug scampering across the kitchen table. Had it been? A bug scurrying across the floor here.

In my sobriety, I'd spent an entire night awake in this attic. No exhaustion or blurred vision had overcome me.

"Chi ... Chi ... Chi."

When I glanced down, in the light, I noticed the soaked pattern of my dress. Floral. The same dress I'd worn on initiation night. Not brown tights and a pair of wings. The same floral dress.

Had I ever left Chi house? Had I ever returned to the dorm to collect my things? I felt like I was losing my mind.

The laughter echoed below again, taunting me, creeping closer. I leapt for the wall and clawed at the fissure until my fingernails pulled back and bled. Then the floor squeaked open, and a voice bellowed from inside.

"Don't you remember your list?" one sister called up.

Another said, "Let's remind her."

Yara's long blonde hair materialized in the shadows, but her face was indistinguishable. "Cockroaches—check. Losing your mind—check. Death?" she giggled. "That's the power of Chi."

Two more sisters appeared and the trio slunk toward me, toward the light, and I could see why their faces were blurred. They wore headdresses of copper, fuzzy black eyes, and protruding antennae. Down their backs were cape-like, transparent wings with veins running through them. Each of their bodies were encased by striped abdomens and jutting, bent legs. More sisters crept up behind them.

They inched closer. Tens of them. I shrieked, but they kept pressing, smothering, rushing me. I turned toward the hole I'd excavated in the wall and jammed my head inside it. Its teeth bit and pulled at my scalp until I burst through. I tumbled onto the awning and, without thinking, scampered for the ledge and slid down one of the columns. I landed on the cement below.

Above me, the X of Chi house loomed, paler than I remembered. I waited for the sisters to descend after me. But all was silent.

In the shattered front door window, my own reflection caught my eye. I was more thin and gray than I remembered. It was as if a stranger stared back.

Then the reflection smiled, even though my own expression had not changed. I drew a hand to my mouth and shuddered. She pointed toward an orange notice in the corner of the window then threw back her head in inaudible laughter.

Condemned. This structure is unsafe and its use or occupancy is prohibited.

It listed Chi house's address. The date stamped was from ten years ago.

I backed away slowly, down the front steps, and into the unforgiving sunshine. The weeds of the overgrown lawn grabbed at my ankles. Decay pockmarked the pale-yellow bricks of the exterior. Its black shutters were unhinged and twisted. Fractured mint green tiles barely clung to the roof.

Then they reappeared. The sisters, now a congregation of roaches, each over five feet tall, peered at me from the hole in the attic above. No more fabric and painted costumes, but the shine of exoskeletons. No more masks, but the bent-neck, elongated faces of bugs.

I blinked hard, but no amount of squinting changed their form. So I turned my back and quickened my pace.

Another student materialized in the distance, walking down the sidewalk. I recognized the sweep of blonde hair, the nearby scent of coconut, the confidence in her stride.

"Yara!" I cried, my voice still hoarse. I sprinted toward her. "Please, help me!"

When I placed a hand on her shoulder, she spun around. The face I expected to be Yara's was another face scrunched in disgust. As I tried to explain, a piercing scream crawled from her bow-shaped lips.

Harvest

As Magnolia unearthed turnips in her grandmother's late-autumn garden, she wondered if she should tell her about the baby. It wasn't that she wanted to keep a secret, especially from her grandmother, after all her kindness. Some things were just too unusual to share, and one had to pick their words carefully.

The thing was she couldn't go home ever again after she'd phoned her parents, letting them know she was pregnant. It was her third year of college. She wouldn't make it to her fourth. They hung up on her. So she drove to her grandmother's house in the countryside because her grandmother had been a nurse and a midwife many years ago. Her grandmother took one look at her suitcase and swollen belly and marched her upstairs to the loft room to unpack.

It was strange how different the estate felt now, how different everything felt. Once upon a time Magnolia wondered when she'd get her own green thumb, just like her grandmother. She wasn't allowed to go in the garden back then, but she'd stare at her grandmother pruning and weeding and deadheading with scissors each time the flowers faded, through the windows of the A-frame house. The one time Magnolia did sneak into the garden, she stole a bright red tomato off the vine and devoured it whole before her grandmother whisked her away to spank her.

Magnolia placed a hand against the cold spot along her abdomen and gazed across her grandmother's garden. It spanned at least 1000 square feet, which her grandmother said was large enough to feed five people year-round. Having worked the earth now for almost a year, she believed it.

That was the exchange. Gardening for room and board. It was Magnolia's suggestion. Her grandmother was reluctant at first.

"But the baby," her grandmother insisted.

But the garden was a shadow. Spanish moss clung to the wraparound porch, where hollyhocks once cascaded. The soil was dry and cracking, almost grayed, as if it were dead skin. Even though Magnolia was heavy and tired and believed she had a brown thumb, she offered to tend it, because somehow things still grew. Among the weeds were the same plump tomatoes she remembered, framed by shimmering green leaves.

"I'll teach you everything I know," her grandmother promised. And she almost had.

Magnolia remembered her first awkward handling of the soil knife, with its one serrated edge and measurements through the center, as she was taught to disembowel weeds by their roots. She'd sliced her arm with the pointed tip. But now she wielded it like a master chef.

The bucket by her feet was full of turnips, bruised purple on their crowns. They'd seeded in late summer so the turnips would be sweeter and more tender at harvest time now. The garden was a place of life and death. This much she knew. As one seed was planted another was harvested. The cucumbers replaced the broccoli. The pumpkins replaced the cucumbers.

And her grandmother's garden seemed to always bloom. It never exhausted, even in winter.

One time, the local newspaper had awarded her grandmother a prize for the best local garden. She'd kept the clipping on the refrigerator for years until it yellowed. Magnolia remembered how they'd asked her grandmother her secret, and she was quoted as saying, coyly, "The secret's in my soil."

Magnolia scraped the soil knife clean against her overalls and stuck it back in its sheath.

"Maggie? Magpie?" her grandmother called from inside the house. "It's time for dinner!"

"Coming!" she shouted back.

Magnolia clutched her garden gloves to her chest and shivered. The overcast skies and biting breeze let her know autumn had arrived. She hated the cold, hated the feeling of it ever since the baby had stopped moving. Hated how the warmth in her gut was extinguished after she'd arrived at the estate.

The baby was so small then, at seventeen weeks, so small and vulnerable it must have sensed her distress. She regretted ignoring its quiet smallness for months, mistaking it for a shared sadness. After all, there was no one to ask about it but her grandmother.

Then her water broke, and the contractions gripped, and her grandmother rushed her to the hospital. But even after she sweat on a gurney for days, there was no baby to show for it. Had the pain deluded her? she'd wondered then. Had it been stillborn? Had her grandmother put it up for adoption?

The doctor released her on the condition she'd return for an examination. She returned alone, insisting her grandmother not bother with the trip, and the doctor poked at her and put his cold stethoscope against every inch of her body. A CT scan revealed the baby was still there, but it wasn't inside of her womb. It was inside her abdomen, trapped, the doctor explained, and calcified. A stone baby. Its blood flow had probably been cut off months ago, and her body couldn't reabsorb the remains. Had she experienced anything strange since the pregnancy started? the doctor had asked.

Magnolia didn't want to tell the country doctor about the baby's sudden quiet, about the cold spot, like winter, she'd felt growing in her belly.

The doctor showed her the blueish 3D image of a monster instead of her baby. Thin limbs and bulbous joints and perforations along the baby's callous skin. Its thick head was turned sideways, as if it was about to take a nap, but its eye sockets were still hollow and covered in skin. Its little baby smile was warped to one side.

The doctor recommended immediate surgical removal, but the out-of-pocket cost was steep. Magnolia already wondered how she would pay for the CT scan without insurance or a job or explaining all of this to her grandmother.

"What happens if I don't remove it?" she'd asked.

The doctor looked at her as if she were crazy. So Magnolia said she'd think it over, even though she had no plan to do so.

"Magpie! Honey, please," her grandmother begged. "Dinner's going to get cold!"

"Coming!" she shouted again and stomped toward the house.

The inside of the kitchen was warm, and Magnolia abandoned her clogs at the door. On the stove sat a large pot. The top frothed as vegetable chunks bubbled to the surface, and an ivory ham bone stuck out of the center. In the kitchen air, the aroma of onions, cloves, and potatoes circled.

"What's this?" she asked.

"Stone soup." Her grandmother clicked down the heat to simmer. "And it's ready. Grab the ladle. Don't be shy." She handed Magnolia an impossibly deep bowl.

There was already a plate of warm biscuits, a tub of butter, a knife, and an apple at her place. Her grandmother knew this was too much.

As Magnolia held the apple, she remembered what the obstetrician at the women's clinic had told her just before she called her parents. "Your baby's the size of an apple . . . or a fist-sized stone."

It had been a running joke between them, the baby growing into a larger and larger stone each time Magnolia visited. The wall chart compared it to food, but the obstetrician knew food was a touchy subject. On the intake form, in the past medical history, Magnolia had checked a single box: eating disorder. It was a simple way of saying everything had been disordered since she'd left home and reaching a finger into the back of her throat was the only way she felt she had control. But the last time she'd done that was the end of freshman year, more than a year before she found out she was pregnant.

Had she turned the baby into stone by calling it that visit after visit? Had she conjured its fate?

Her grandmother nudged the golden biscuits in her direction. "You aren't eating," she said. "Everything okay?"

Magnolia took one, but only picked it apart. "I'll be fine."

They swallowed their soup, spoonful by spoonful, until Magnolia's teeth clamped down on what felt like a ham bone. She spit into her napkin, where a dark gray shard materialized instead.

"Did you really put stones in your stone soup?" She showed the rock fragment to her grandmother.

"Sure. I get them from the garden. A piece must've broken off." Magnolia put down her spoon and turned her cheek. Her grandmother cast a disapproving glance. "What? I ran it through the dishwasher yesterday. The recipe calls for it. It's for flavor, and it prevents things from settling at the bottom of the pot where they can burn." Magnolia crossed her arms. "You need to eat. Stop picking at that biscuit. This would've never happened if you hadn't—"

"Gotten knocked up?"

Her grandmother's expression went flat. "No, God, no. That happens to women all the time." She took a long, deep breath. "All I'm saying is if you hadn't done that to your body—starved it—you would've been strong enough to carry the baby full term. You were so thin that first year of school, Magpie. So thin it was like seeing a ghost."

"It was years ago, Grandma. I don't do that anymore, and not once since I stepped foot in your house."

Magnolia lost her appetite and excused herself from the table, still tonguing the tender spot where the rock shard had slit her gums.

That night, she woke about an hour before dawn and couldn't fall back to sleep. Insomnia had been a constant uninvited guest, given the stress and the pregnancy. Her grandmother's tendency to wake at all hours and fuss didn't help. Starting the dishwasher at 4 a.m. Vacuuming the staircase at midnight. Magnolia couldn't really blame her for this, though. Her grandmother wasn't used to having a roommate.

She stared at the picture of a hedgehog hanging on the wall across from her bed. At the top of the frame were two hedgehogs, one snuffing through grass and another balled-up beside it. Below, on a backdrop of black, were floating, disembodied hedgehog parts. A skull, two teeth, two paws cut off at the wrists, an iris and pupil, and a single quill. The painting also had what appeared to be a skinned baby hedgehog, with bands of red, fleshy tendons and a pig-like face.

It was a peculiar decoration for a kid's room, Magnolia thought. She remembered how it gave her nightmares when she was younger. She'd once asked her grandmother to cover it with a blanket. But now she thought it cute in some ways and, given her grandmother's medical background and love of nature, it made more sense.

Her stomach growled from too little dinner, but she hesitated to go downstairs. She didn't want to wake her grandmother, whose ears always seemed to be listening, especially when Magnolia was in the bathroom. She turned toward the window overlooking the garden and thought of the tomatoes, so juicy and ripe. A few still hung from the vine, ready to pluck, and her mouth watered at the sight. It would be a shame to let them shrivel instead of savoring them, she thought.

She slipped on her robe and tiptoed downstairs, where her grandmother's snores echoed behind the closed bedroom door. She wiggled on her clogs and stepped into the moonlight.

Outside, she breathed in the cool air and exhaled steam. She spotted one of the fat, dangling tomatoes and walked over to the vine to pluck it off. As her teeth sank into it, she felt the tender flesh rip apart and the insides spill across her tongue. The saltiness stung the wound in her gums, but she didn't care. The juices overfilled her mouth and dribbled down her chin.

As she chewed, she noticed a soft white glow in the garden's corner, beyond the row of beanstalks. The wind whistled past her ears. She expected to see a dead possum or rotting cantaloupe. But the wind smelled clean, free of decay, as it had most days.

The shape of it became clearer as she approached. Domed top. Three holes on the front. It was a skull. Magnolia gazed at it for several moments, unsure what to do. Why had she not seen it in the garden before? It seemed fake, plastic even, like a Halloween decoration, because it was too clean and undisturbed. She glanced to her right and left then bent down closer. An owl hooted from far away. The skull's hollow eye sockets, drenched in blue moonlight, reminded her of the baby's eyes on the CT scan, and she cupped her lower abdomen instinctively. Then she noticed a small, gray rock clenched between the skull's teeth. The rock was like the one her grandmother had used in the stone soup, but smoother and iridescent.

She plucked it from the jaw and felt the strangest sensation in her belly, like a kick. The baby kicked once and again. Not tiny butterfly flutters like she'd felt earlier in the pregnancy, but jabs. Over and over. Pain. Hunger pangs.

She lifted the rock to her lips and swallowed it whole.

It felt worse going down than her giant prenatal vitamins. But she resisted the urge to choke it back up. As the stone pulled deeper into her stomach, the kicks calmed to gentle nudges. The baby seemed satisfied. She stroked her belly with her fingertips and noted the glow within, the way it now matched the rest of her skin's temperature.

She kept moving her hands between the cold, lifeless skull and her warm, stirring stomach in disbelief. Maybe the doctor had been wrong. Maybe the baby was still alive. Already she wondered when she'd feel it moving again or if her grandmother would believe her. It made no sense, she knew. The thought of her grandmother saying it was all in her head, that even the best medicine and doctors couldn't bring a stone baby back to life, both angered and terrified her. She knew the spot in her abdomen was growing warmer. She could touch it now and know.

Behind her, a creaking door echoed. She jumped, afraid it was her grandmother. But the sound didn't come from the house. It was nearer the tomato vines. That's when she noticed the shed door swaying in the breeze.

She tucked the skull under her arm and headed back. At first, she thought she'd forgotten to latch the door earlier in the day, when her grandmother called for dinner. Then she realized the bucket, soil knife, and garden gloves had been set out for her already. Perhaps her grandmother had forgotten to latch the door instead.

There was an object preventing the door from closing. A box the size of a ripe pumpkin. But it was square and black and ordinary. There was no latch or keyhole, just dust and grime on top of the lid. She wondered how often she'd passed it by when tending the grounds.

She tipped the lid to reveal stacks of newspaper clippings and random trinkets. Bits of fabric, a badge with her grandmother's maiden name on it, a broken pair of spectacles. It was too dark to read the articles, so she locked the shed door and headed back inside with both the box and skull.

In the loft, she turned on the lamp, which was dim but sufficient to read. The newspaper clipping on top was the one she remembered about her grandmother winning a local best garden award. As she dug deeper, she found several articles from her grandmother's past, when she worked at a women's hospital then a psychiatric facility. Apparently, they'd been in the same building.

Magnolia paused to read one titled "Women's Hospital Shut

Down After Infant Deaths." It gave no clear explanation for the deaths. Most of the babies were premature and unable to be resuscitated when their hearts suddenly stopped. An examiner was called in and suspended them, citing newly credentialed doctors with little experience, poor funding, and too little nursing staff as the cause. The county announced that all births would now take place at a larger hospital in town, at least an hour's drive away.

From the looks of the other articles, her grandmother stayed at the old facility after it was stripped of its purpose and refashioned into a psychiatric hospital. Magnolia remembered how her grandmother didn't like to speak about her time there.

The clippings also had titles about missing patients. Six women within the span of a year. Dawn and Terry and Ellen. One of the women even had a glass eye of green, an article said.

Magnolia held the skull up toward the dissection of the hedgehogs. The shapes were different, but they were the same ivory hue. Both blanched and weathered bones. She wondered what a glass eye would look like inside of one of those sockets.

"Magpie? Are you awake?" her grandmother called from downstairs.

She slipped the skull and box underneath her bed.

"I woke to pee and couldn't fall back asleep," she lied.

"Well then come down here," she said. "I'll fry up some eggs, and we can get started. The first frost is coming, which means dead veggies if we don't get them all out of there."

Magnolia glanced out the window, realizing the pink light of dawn had appeared, and shuffled downstairs.

* * *

The stone baby's feet tickled Magnolia's abdomen again just before dinnertime. She wanted to shower and rest after the harvesting that day, but she felt the spot grow from tepid to summery and knew it would have to wait.

"Grandma? Do you have more of that stone soup from last night?"

"Plenty," her grandmother said.

"Can we reheat it for dinner again tonight?"

Her grandmother cocked her head. "I thought you hated it, though."

"I reconsidered," said Magnolia. "It's quick, and I'm hungry. I don't think I can wait."

"Well, hunger will do that to you. I'll go inside and heat it up, but I'll remove the stone this time."

"No!" The baby kicked her hard from inside, and Magnolia had to keep her composure. "Keep the stone. It wouldn't taste the same without it, as you said."

Her grandmother shrugged. "Well, let's get a fresh stone then. One that's not prone to breaking apart. You pick it out while I start the stove?"

Magnolia nodded her head.

Once her grandmother was back inside, Magnolia bent forward to whisper. "Okay, baby. You're the one who's hungry. Help me choose the stone."

She wandered through the rows for several minutes, picking up rocks, big and small, while the baby kept mostly still. On the edge of the garden, not too far from where she'd found the skull, she noticed a rugged slab about as wide as her grandmother's cooking pot. She picked it up and felt feet drumming against her insides.

"Okay, that's the one then."

But as Magnolia turned to leave, she noticed a collection of smaller, colorless rocks buried in the stone slab's impression. She set the stone aside and dug around the individual rocks with the pointed tip of the soil knife. The rocks became longer until they almost connected. When she was done, a hand shape sat atop of the remaining soil. These weren't stones either, but more bones. She glanced back at the house to make sure her grandmother wasn't watching then scooped each individual bone into her pockets.

Before she grabbed the slab again, she pocketed a palm-sized limestone at the base of the fence, believing this might buy her some time when the next craving hit. The baby sent soft, comforting waves through her belly to show its approval.

At dinner, Magnolia helped herself to seconds and thirds of the soup while her grandmother watched in awe. The soup tasted like dirt, calcium, and iron and gave her the warmest feeling she'd had in her belly yet.

"What?" Magnolia asked, pausing to peek up.

"I was just wondering if you were hungry enough for dessert tonight, too. But I think I have my answer."

Magnolia nodded her head, and her grandmother went to cut some cake.

As they ate, Magnolia realized the cake didn't sit as well as the stone soup. She went back to her routine of picking her food apart and spreading it across her plate.

She thought back to the box of articles hidden beneath her bed and to the collection of bones in her pockets. "Tell me about the time you worked in the women's hospital, Grandma."

At first her grandmother hesitated. "Are you sure you want to hear stories about babies when—?" She gestured to her own abdomen.

"Yes," Magnolia insisted. "It might make me feel better."

For a while she let her grandmother ramble on about birth plans, prenatal examinations, the when's and how's of the hospital's transition to a mental institution, and one time when they'd nearly lost a baby after his circumcision.

"Did any babies die?" Magnolia asked. "Did any of their moms?"

Her grandmother frowned. "I suppose so. After all, it was a hospital. We didn't have all the things medicine has now." She took a long sip of her tea and turned her face toward the window that overlooked the garden. "But you don't want to hear about those babies, Magpie."

"But what about—"

"I'm sorry, sweetie, but I'm really tired after all that work in the garden. Aren't you?" she asked. "It's time we each shower and get some rest. Tomorrow, we start canning."

Magnolia lowered her gaze. "How come you never ask about the baby? Or what the doctor said when I went back?"

Her grandmother grabbed their bowls and placed them in the sink. "You'll tell me when you're ready. Won't you, Magpie?"

In bed that night, Magnolia stared up at the hedgehog painting and sucked on the limestone she'd pocketed earlier. This gave her an idea. When her grandmother's gentle snoring floated up from the lower floor, she slunk down from bed and arranged the bones from the garden until they formed a hand again. Some pieces looked misplaced or backwards, perhaps, but she'd finished the jigsaw. The hand was petite and feminine, like her own. She wondered what color flesh it would be, imagined the lines across the knuckles and palm, the length of the fingernails, their color, if the hand was more of a Dawn or Terry or Ellen. She wondered if this hand had felt a baby moving inside of it, too.

She reached under the bed for the articles and perused them again. Dawn was a mother whose premature baby passed unexpectedly in the middle of the night. The others were two of the six patients who disappeared at the mental hospital, both no older than 22 years old. One had severe depression and one had schizophrenia. Investigators initially believed the depressed patient took her own life out in the woods behind the hospital, but a body was never found. The other was believed to have wandered off. But the odd thing—the detail that opened the investigation—was that both patients needed a key to get out of the facility. Only the doctors and nurses had keys. Her grandmother would have had one.

The dates seemed to coincide. While her grandmother worked at the each of the facilities, babies and women went missing. Was her grandmother involved? she wondered.

A wave of heat rushed over her then, like a hot flash, originating in her belly. Perspiration beaded above her lip and made her pajamas stick. Relief only came when she started gnawing on the limestone. She chewed so hard she thought the enamel would come off her teeth.

Then she heard a clang downstairs. She quickly extinguished the lamplight and grabbed the soil knife on her nightstand. The sound of footsteps traveled through the lower hallway and into the kitchen. A door creaked open, and below her bedroom window, she saw her grandmother walking toward the shed.

The baby kicked. "Not now, baby," she whispered. She bent down to shove everything under the bed. By the time she peered through the window again, her grandmother had disappeared.

She continued to suck on the stone as she put on her robe and slippers. She pressed the soil knife against her hip and tiptoed downstairs. When she passed by her grandmother's bedroom door, she heard nothing. She walked to the kitchen, and no one was there either, but the door was ajar.

She stepped into the dark and glanced around without finding her grandmother. She tossed the limestone aside. Her abdomen started to sizzle. "Shh. Shh," she told the baby. "Now's not the time." She felt as if it would burn a hole through her skin.

"Grandma?" she called out. "Are you here?"

A figure jostled in the moonlight between a cobweb of green bean vines and an empty, pockmarked row. Magnolia gripped the soil knife. Then the white of her grandmother's hair manifested. She was digging through the dirt with both hands.

"Grandma?"

"Oh, God!" she screamed. "What are you doing out here at this hour? I thought you were asleep!"

"I thought you were asleep, too," Magnolia said. "But I heard noises." She clutched at her belly and hoped nightfall hid the pain on her face, the trickles of sweat along her neck.

"I was looking for the soil knife. I thought I'd had it earlier today. Did you see it anywhere? I can't even find the pouch."

Magnolia hesitated. "Can't that wait until morning?"

Her grandmother sighed. "You're probably right. I just don't want to lose it. I'd have to drive all the way into the city to get another. If it got buried in snow, it'd be ruined."

"Let me look for it tomorrow while I clean up the garden," she offered. "I'm sure it was just misplaced."

"You're a dear, Magpie. Yes. Now help this old woman get up off her old knees!"

Magnolia steadied her grandmother and pushed her back toward the house. Before they left the garden, she bent down and picked up a handful of pebbles and slipped them into the folds of her robe.

Inside, she helped her grandmother into bed and dimmed the light. "I shouldn't have spent so much time in the garden today. My whole body is stiff."

"Goodnight, Grandma." Magnolia gave her a kiss on the cheek.

Her grandmother pressed a hand to her face. "You're burning up," she said. "Are you sick? Your face is flushed."

"I'm overdressed. Flannel pjs and a robe? What was I thinking? It's not that cold yet. I'll open the window upstairs, and I'll be fine."

She closed her grandmother's bedroom door. Then she reached into her pocket and devoured the handful of pebbles.

* * *

When the sun hit Magnolia's face the next morning, she felt sticky and hot. The pillow and the bed sheet were soggy, as if she'd had a fever dream. In a panic, she grabbed her stomach but still felt the diluted heat of the stone baby under her skin. She relaxed. Then the smell of coffee wafted up to her nostrils.

"Magpie? Breakfast!"

Magnolia had no interest in what was cooking downstairs. She searched through the pockets of her robe until she found traces of crushed pebble and dirt. She palmed them into her mouth and licked the fabric clean. Then she smoothed out her hair and changed into her denim overalls. The soil knife was hung against her thigh, hidden by a thin belt she'd strapped on underneath the overalls.

"No breakfast?" her grandmother asked as Magnolia tried to slip past her.

More than anything, she needed to get to the garden and the stones. "Maybe a glass of water," she said. "But I'll take it with me to the garden. Got to get to work before the first frost comes, you know? Get all those dead things into the compost. Oh, and find the soil knife."

She filled up a thermos of water and excused herself.

With her back turned to the house, she used the soil knife to shave the earth's crust until rocks emerged. She popped each one into her mouth. The heat in her belly began to cool.

She navigated to the spot where she'd found her grandmother last night. The dirt looked as if an animal had tried to bury something there—or dig it up. She was afraid to dig deeper, unsure what she might find. She put the soil knife in its sheath and burrowed with her garden gloves. Luscious gray stones cascaded into the hollow, and she couldn't help but eat those, too. The rocks became gravellier as she dug, and she relished the abrasiveness against her tongue. The baby kicked and kicked until she was salivating, stuffing handfuls of dirt into her mouth. Then she bit down on a substance so hard she thought she'd broken one of her teeth. When she swished saliva in her mouth, she thought she felt the fractured tooth banging around.

But she felt no pain, not like a cracked tooth would feel. Something thick and smooth remained as well. She tongued it and discerned a hollowed-out half-sphere, like a seashell.

She spit beside the hole once then twice. Two teeth with fang-like roots fell out then what looked like another warped evil eye marble. She lifted it and examined it closer. The eye was green. First the skull, then a hand, teeth, and an eyeball. A glass eyeball. In her mouth.

Magnolia recoiled and vomited, but the bile wouldn't stop coming. The sound of her retching eventually drew her grandmother out of the house.

"Magpie? You okay? What's happening? I told you that you were sick!"

Magnolia covered the teeth and glass eye with her left hand as her grandmother leaned over her shoulder. She heaved twice more. When she was done, her grandmother grabbed her face and examined it.

"Is that dirt coming from your mouth? Oh my God." Her grandmother sprang to her feet. "I knew something was wrong. I *knew* it!" She paced the garden rows. "You don't just go into labor and not give birth." Her voice raised, "Look what you did to the baby, Magnolia! There's parasites and bacteria and all kinds of toxic things in that soil. How could you?"

Magnolia spit the acidic juices out of her cheeks one more time then wiped her mouth with the garden glove. She could feel the baby pulse inside of her. It felt like a boiling heartbeat. Sweat dripped from the pores of her forehead and underneath her breasts. She gripped the teeth and eyeball in her left hand.

Her grandmother kept shouting. "I taught you everything I knew about gardening, and you betrayed my trust! Well, no more. This is over. You hear me? Tonight you pack your bags and tomorrow I'll drive you to the bus stop." She started sobbing. "I can't believe you did this. You're sick! Sick in the head!"

A drop of perspiration oozed down Magnolia's nose. "You're sick, too," she whispered.

"What was that?"

Her grandmother turned around and gasped at the sight of Magnolia. She was drenched, lava hot, and sweltering from the baby's throbs. It banged against her flesh, begging to get out. Magnolia blinked back sweat as she lifted her left palm to her grandmother's face.

Her grandmother's eyes widened at the glistening teeth and eyeball. Her jaw fell open. "No," she whispered. "No. Where did you find that?"

"I trusted *you*," Magnolia hissed. "They all did. That box in the shed? I saw the articles. I know what happened to them!"

The heat from her abdomen clawed into her brain and lit it on fire. She recalled the painting on her bedroom wall then. The fleshy baby hedgehog, so cute and coiled upon itself. She dropped the teeth and glass eye and unmasked the soil knife. Sweat dribbled from her fingertips onto its serrated blade.

"No, Magpie. Please don't kill your grandmother," she begged. "I'll do anything."

Magnolia stepped toward her. "This is for Dawn and Terry and all the women," she said, "who weren't crazy at all. Who just wanted to see their babies alive!"

Her grandmother fell to her knees. "Please!"

Then Magnolia turned the tip of the blade toward her stomach, pierced the skin, and sliced from hip to hip. Her grandmother screamed in horror as the calcified backbone of the baby emerged through the wound. And as the small, decayed mouth yawned open, Magnolia felt her fever break.

Those Who Wish to be Clean

The forecast called for rain again, which meant Nell had to keep the children inside. From the eighth floor window of their apartment, she could see the playground peering back, as soaked and sad as a kitten abandoned in a storm. Green paint peeled back from the bars. The colors of the wooden spinner turned anemic, and frayed rubber swings swayed over puddles of muddied water, a mist rolling in through the darkness. It wasn't abandoned yet, per se. Just neglected, like everything else in the trio of apartments that hugged the playground. Their gray faces matched the endless clouds and bled through with red rust stains.

Children had never been part of Nell's plan until her husband came along. Dirty hands, dirty mouths, touching every surface. But he wanted them. He wanted to have as many children as they could before they turned thirty. He even insisted on changing their diapers.

But now Simone was five and Kenny was three, and Nell was the only one who had made it to thirty years old. He drowned when his vehicle fell into a sinkhole, leaving her a widowed mother. She couldn't wait for the day the kids were tall enough to see over the top of the washer or big enough to push the vacuum cleaner with their own bare hands. Parenthood exhausted her in the same way her pregnancies had, with aching joints and mood swings that bordered on breakdowns. Then there was the guilt—the mother's guilt—for even thinking badly of her children.

Nell turned from the window and stepped on a pair of dirty socks.

"Someone come pick up these socks, please," she called down the narrow hallway. Nell heard the tired in her voice echo off the apartment walls.

The clamor of little feet on the hardwood neared. "Sorry, Mom," Kenny whispered at the floor. He picked up the socks and scurried off.

Nell shook her head. Her kids were afraid of her, and she didn't know how to stop it. This was what being a single parent and afraid of their messes got her, a contagious cycle of despair. Every time she tried to apologize, another eyesore manifested, and the itch of correcting her children was impossible to resist.

Nell peeked around the corner of the kids' room and saw them playing with Legos.

Sensing her presence, Simone glanced over her shoulder. "Can we play outside today?"

"Afraid not, honey. It's raining again."

Simone pouted. "I still don't get why we can't play in the rain."

"Cause it's wet," Kenny told her matter-of-factly.

Nell stifled a chuckle. "Maybe tomorrow. Mommy's going to take a shower. Be good, okay?"

Simone and Kenny nodded, and Nell disappeared into the bathroom.

Being clean was Nell's favorite feeling. She remembered as a child when she started doing chores around the house. Her own mother praised her for her spotless laundry, her mirror-finish polishing skills. It gave her pleasure to clean. So when her husband died, she leaned on the one skill she had and loved and became a cleaning lady to pay the rent.

She didn't know what it was like for the other cleaning ladies in these parts. But one "in" with a friend who knew a family uptown, and she was booking regulars throughout the week. An hour here. Half a day there. Freshly shampooed carpets. Suffering the pungent smell of bleach to behold immaculate tile grout. Sometimes she'd be the referral for a move-out—a one woman show—or entrusted with sanitizing after a particularly grimy tenant. The before-and-afters gave her heart as much of a rush as it did the owners. Although the pay, in general, wasn't much, Nell was tipped well.

Then there was home. Chaos buried in the carpets, finger-smudged surfaces, sheets and chairs and clothes in disarray. She would gladly pay someone else to clean it if she had the money. But it all went to keeping the lights on and food in everyone's mouths. Even the babysitting was provided as a favor by a neighbor on their floor, Miss Mildred, who Nell immediately liked when they met years ago. Mildred's couch was still covered in plastic and visitors were expected to keep their sodas on the coasters. Nell cleaned Mildred's apartment once each week in exchange for childcare. Plus Mildred sometimes dropped off dinner, which was plentiful and delicious and made Nell feel obligated to scrub extra hard just to deserve it.

Otherwise, Nell's own apartment was no calling card for her profession. Perhaps that's why she retreated to the bathroom when she could. Minimal damage happened there. Clean-ups were easy when they did. The possibility of mold, which she could control, was greater than the possibility of children's gunk, which she could only control so much. In the shower, with the children just far enough out of sight, Nell felt her responsibilities and worries wash away with the soap suds.

Nell saw it growing darker outside as she pulled a towel from the linen closet. Having a bathroom with just a shower seemed counterintuitive to raising babies, but the idea of swimming in her own skin cells in a bath made her want to vomit. When they apartment hunted for the first time, she made that clear to her husband. Instead, they bought a plastic baby bath for the sink when Simone arrived and a bigger one later that fit in the shower. Simone was now almost at the age where she'd be able to bathe unattended, and Nell counted down the days and up the inches until that blissful moment arrived.

Nell stripped off her shirt and turned on the showerhead. Her forearm stung in the ice-cold stream. Because of the old plumbing in the apartment complex, it took several minutes for hot water to reach the eighth floor. She used the remainder of the time to finish undressing and check her business email on her cell phone.

When Nell was finally beneath the hot running water, she felt like she lost her mind. In a good way, a daydreaming kind of way. She imagined she was beneath a giant waterfall on a deserted tropical island. The pounding of the drops against her skin and the tile muted out the shouts of children playing in the shared playground below their apartment, honking traffic, and the clamor of nearby trains. Today it would mute the thunder as well and its threatening hiss above the city.

The water flowed from Nell's crown to her toes and steamed up the glass door. There was minimal chance Simone and Kenny would burst through the mist. They had before, and her response had been so uncontrolled and harsh, they knew better than to do it again. It was as if her anger broke the lack-of-privacy spell all toddlers seemed to be under. Yet she regretted also knowing the apartment might catch on fire, and they'd be waiting outside the door patiently until she finished.

Nell grabbed the shampoo and lathered up her hair. She watched the suds trickle down her breasts and over the stretch marks along her stomach. The drain frothed up momentarily with suds, and Nell noted that she'd need to pour clog gel down it after she was done.

The buzz of the hot water made her skin flush, and its heat deadened her cares. She breathed in the vapors.

Then a scream curled up through the streams of water and vibrated in her ears.

Nell gasped. "Simone? Kenny?" she yelled.

The water continued to rush.

She turned off the shower head, wrapped a towel around her torso, and burst into the living room. There, Simone and Kenny sat watching television, Legos sprinkled around the base of the couch.

"Who put all those—?" Nell caught herself. "Did one of you scream?"

Nell turned toward the television. Their favorite characters, a mouse and a duck, were in a sailboat headed toward an island. Nell had seen this episode many times before. There was no screaming. Just adventure and a sing-along at the end.

"Did one of you scream?" Nell repeated, trying to calm her voice. But her nerves rattled in her throat, and she could tell from their faces that Simone and Kenny thought she was mad at them. They stared at her dripping hair and the water puddling beneath her feet.

"Okay then. Well," Nell whispered to herself. "I just thought . . ." She cleared her throat. "Mommy's going to finish her shower now."

She sloshed back down the hallway toward the bathroom, trying not to slip.

* * *

The rain stopped on Tuesday, and Nell was relieved to find the kids and Miss Mildred already dressed for the park when she came home from work. As Simone and Kenny danced toward the playground wedged between the three dilapidated apartment buildings, Mildred confessed she'd given them candy an hour ago.

The park was practically empty. The bars were still slick from rain earlier that day, and the sky was still overcast, but Nell needed the kids to run off their extra energy because she needed a quiet afternoon.

An unexpected white glove inspection followed her work today. A frowning customer, convinced he'd asked her to deep clean the shower when he hadn't, refused to pay her until she promised to come back tomorrow and finish. She cursed herself for not itemizing her services and being desperate for the cash.

As Simone and Kenny ran circles around the swings, a few more children from the complexes appeared, some in their hoodies, some in galoshes. She watched them grab hands and swing around, then race from one building to another, shouting "Tag!". She was happy to see Simone and Kenny excited for once this week, but also hopeful that they'd barely have the energy to make it through their dinner.

A couple appeared on the opposite end of Nell's bench and

silently watched the children play. The man was older, with a rugged beard and spectacles. He wore a tan boating hat with a long chin strap that dangled onto his belly. It was hard to tell the woman's age. Her hair was such pale blonde, it could have passed for gray, and it frizzed in the heat like a bird's nest. She pulled at the hair closest to her face, as if she were nervous, and stared across the playground with milky blue eyes.

"They're harmless," Nell said to the woman, as if to apologize, as if her own rambunctious children were the ones making the woman agitated. "A friend gave them candy before I picked them up today."

The couple both turned toward her.

"My name is Nell. I live in apartment 8C." She raised a friendly hand toward the couple but pulled it back when she realized no one was offering theirs. Nell and Mildred had talked about this many times before. Race over poverty. Even living in these tattered buildings didn't erase that. She hated how they looked at her as if she was dirty. "You all just move in?"

The couple shook their heads yes in unison.

"Sorry," the woman said, pointing at Nell's folded hands. "I have a compromised immune system. Germs and all. I'd rather not shake hands."

Nell could respect that.

"We moved in just below you," said the man, quite a bit more chipper than the woman with him. "7C. This is my wife, Helena, and I'm Carl."

"Pleasure to meet you both," Nell said. "Is that one yours?" She pointed to a pale, blonde boy in overalls playing with Simone and Kenny.

The couple shook their heads no. Carl even laughed.

Nell waited an uncomfortable minute for them to point to

their child. When they didn't, she asked, "Do you all have any children?"

Helena crinkled her nose. "No. They get sick so often. I just couldn't," she said in disgust.

Nell bit her tongue before she blurted out, *Then why the hell are you two sitting in a dirty kids' playground?*

She shifted on the bench and searched the playground for Simone and Kenny, who had disappeared up a ladder and into a crawl tunnel with the pale boy.

"Can I ask you something, Nell?" Carl said. "It's Nell, right?"

Nell shook her head yes.

"Have you been baptized?"

Nell glared. "Beg your pardon?"

Carl chuckled and wrapped an arm around Helena. "It's only fair. You ask us a really personal question, then we get to ask you one. So have you been baptized?"

"That's none of your business."

The laughter fell from his face. "There's still time, Nell." His eyes turned from her and stared blankly at the children on the playground.

Nell got up from the bench and stomped over to her kids just as it began to sprinkle again. "Come on. Time for dinner," she said, grabbing them each by a hand.

They scurried past the couple as thunder rumbled in the distance.

Inside, Nell put on a pot to heat and told the children to wash up. She cursed the couple as she poured in salt, brought the water to a boil, and tossed in the pasta. First a terrible client. Now a terrible neighbor.

For her part, she also ruined dinner. The sauce was too watery. Simone kept stirring hers into the noodles, as if she'd hoped that would thicken it. Kenny just put down his fork and rested his head in his hands.

"Sorry the rain stopped playtime again, you two. Sorry dinner wasn't so great."

Simone held up her hands. "Can we watch another *Tales from the—from the—*?"

"*Crypt?*" Nell asked.

"Yeah. I promise to not have nightmares this time."

Nell realized Simone was too young to handle the show, but one night when Simone couldn't sleep, she joined Nell in the living room. Nell thought Simone fell asleep before the scary parts even started. But that belief was put to rest when Simone crawled into her bed a couple hours later.

"Mommy really needs her sleep tonight. Maybe this weekend."

Simone moaned and put her head in her hands, too.

After the kids were tucked in bed, Nell washed up the dinner plates and switched to her pajamas. The sky still rumbled outside the windows, and she could hear the finger-tapping sound of raindrops against the windowpanes. She was tired, and the thought of returning to that cranky man's house tomorrow to clean weighed her down. But the money.

Nell peered through the window blinds. Streams of rain seemed to slow as they barreled through the lights across the street. She noticed one of the lights above the playground darkened. Trees swished and swayed in the wind around it. From under one of the swaying trees, two figures appeared. They held hands as they walked toward her apartment building, the rain continuing to fall upon them. One in a raincoat, the other covered by a wide-brimmed hat.

Just before they reached the edge of the playground, they

stopped and glanced up. A pair of spectacles and two icy blue eyes fixated on her window. Nell covered her mouth and stepped back, letting the tiny slit between the window blinds clamp shut. The words of Carl replayed in her head. *There's still time, Nell.* She turned the lamplight off.

In the bathroom, as she brushed her teeth, Nell noticed a red ring around the sink drain, still wet and oozing upward. A gurgling sound erupted from the drain, as if sludge was caught inside. Nell wondered if the children had tampered with it, or worse, if her own hair or toothpaste had created a clog.

She wiped her fingers along the edge of the drain and pinched them against her thumb.

Blood.

She pulled at the pop-up stopper until it broke free of the flange and eyed into the darkness of the drain.

Suddenly the scream she'd heard in the shower the other day bubbled up from the drain. Faintly this time. It was a child's voice, just as it had been in the shower. A piercing, desperate scream. Any mother would have known, would have shuddered at the sound.

Nell grabbed her cell phone and flipped on the flashlight. She peeped down into the drain, expecting to find more blood or hear more screams. Instead, two glistening eyeballs peered up at her.

Nell cried out and dropped her phone on the floor. She stuck the stopper back inside the drain and covered it with her hands. After whispering to herself for several minutes, she loosened her grip and opened her eyes. "You're seeing things, Nell. Get it together," she told her reflection in the mirror. "Call Mildred. She'll talk some sense into you."

Mildred picked up on the first ring. "Nell? Everything okay?"

"I don't know, Mildred," she sighed into the phone. "Have you heard any strange noises tonight?"

Mildred thought. "It's an old building. What exactly do you mean?"

"Have you met the new couple who moved into 7C?" Nell asked. "I just saw them earlier this week and . . . I don't know what to make of them. I don't think I like them. They kind of creeped me out. They weren't very nice to me when we saw each other at the playground."

"Can't say I have," Mildred confessed. "But, Nell, you don't have to like everyone in this building."

Nell stumbled over her next thought and pulled at her hair. "Mildred. Some strange things have been happening. First I think I hear one of the kids screaming when I'm in the shower. But they weren't. Then I find a ring of blood around the sink drain, and then—then—you're going to think I'm crazy. I swear. I just saw eyeballs looking at me from inside the sink drain."

Mildred was quiet for several moments. "You watch too many horror movies, Nell."

"No, but I—"

"And that red ring around the drain is not blood. It's iron from the municipal water supply. Even I get those stains from time to time."

Nell sighed. This wasn't going well at all. But Mildred was talking sense, as predicted.

"Will you do me a favor, honey?" Mildred asked.

"What?"

"Will you accept my apologies again for giving the kids candy? Then letting them wear you out so much you're starting to see and hear things past midnight? And would you please, for the love of God, Nell, stop watching *Tales from the Crypt* before bed?"

Nell felt like an idiot. "Yes, Mildred. I'm sorry if I woke you."

"You didn't," she replied, "and I promise not to wake you. Now get some rest."

Nell hung up the phone.

In the bathroom, upon second glance, the spot now mimicked rust. A red-orange crayon line drawn around the drain. Mildred was right. Perhaps Nell was letting her imagination run away with her. Perhaps she was searching for a distraction from the real horror of having to clean that man's house a second time tomorrow.

She resisted the urge to check the windows again, to see if Carl and Helena were still out there in the rain. Instead, she tiptoed past the children's bedroom toward her own bed.

* * *

"Have you been baptized in the blood of the Lord?" a stranger, holding a bible above his head, shouted at Nell. She pushed away the flyer he tried to force upon her and headed down the stairs toward the subway. This was the last thing she needed after finishing her cleaning today. The gruff client gave her the money he owed, but not without threatening to leave a bad review on every social media platform where her business existed. Then her vehicle broke down as she left suburbia, and she had to call a tow truck. Fortunately, there was a mechanic in the city who could take her. But the repairs would take a few days and cut into the money she'd just been paid.

Nell flung her wet umbrella onto the seat next to her so no one would sit there. As the train popped in and out of the city, in and out of darkness and rain, the majority of the passengers exited. Nell hadn't taken this line in years but knew her stop would be the last. If she had her way, she'd never venture out this far again for a job, let alone twice for the same client. She stood and made her way toward the doors.

As the train pulled into the next to last station, Nell caught sight of Carl and Helena, standing on the platform. The blue eyes and spectacles whizzed past as the train came to a stop. They faced the train with smiles frozen on their faces, as if looking for and expecting to see her—or at least someone they knew. She gasped and ducked behind some seats at the far end of the car.

"You okay lady?" a man asked, peeking from behind his newspaper.

"Everything's fine," she told him. She whispered it to herself again several times.

The couple couldn't be but one car length away from her. Had they seen her? Would they come? She crawled toward the exit to the next train car, hoping to put more space between her and them.

She opened the exit door and, while balancing on the connection, the train hitched into motion again. She slipped into the next car and hunched over in the closest seat.

Nell pulled at her hair as she tried to think of what to do at the next stop. She'd wait, she decided. She'd wait until the very last minute, until it seemed as if the doors were about to close. Then she'd keep behind them as they walked to their building. She'd wait for the next elevator, too. In movies, the person following, able to watch without being seen, was the one who had the advantage.

The final stop was announced. A handful of figures made

their way to the platform from other train cars. Then just as the doors quivered, Nell slipped out.

She must have waited long enough, she figured, because she didn't see any couples climbing the stairs to the street above. No wide-brimmed hats bobbing along the sidewalk. No shadows at the base of the apartment building.

As the elevator door closed and rose past the seventh floor without any sign of the couple, Nell breathed a sigh of relief. The apartment smelled of chicken pot pie when she opened the door. Simone and Kenny stopped playing and waved at her.

On the kitchen counter was a note: *Be right back*, in Mildred's handwriting. Nell was soaked from walking from the station to the apartment without her umbrella. She threw her thin coat into the washing machine and changed into her robe.

"Where's Miss Mildred?" she asked, somewhat perturbed that the children were left alone.

"There's a leak in her apartment," Simone explained. "Someone called. She said she'd be right back."

"I see. Well, did you all get a chance to eat already? It smells great in here."

Simone and Kenny nodded their heads.

"One for you," Kenny said. He pointed at the refrigerator.

Nell removed a serving of chicken pot pie and microwaved it until it was steaming. It was 15 more minutes before her head returned. The kids were watching cartoons from one of their favorite series, the mouse and the duck on the sailboat again. Still no Miss Mildred.

"How long has Miss Mildred been gone?" Nell asked.

Simone shrugged her shoulders. "I don't know."

"How many times have you all watched that show since she left?"

Simone and Kenny glanced at each other and calculated.

"Three? Maybe four," Simone said. "Yeah. Four times with you here."

Nell knew by heart that the episode was thirty minutes. This meant Mildred had left the children alone for almost two hours. She checked her phone screen.

Plumbing problems. Mess all over the floor or I'd bring the kids with me.

And then, half an hour later: *They're okay. I checked on them. Left my number. Let me know when you are back.*

Nell texted Mildred that she'd returned, then sunk her head into her hands and let out a sigh.

"Hey, Mom. Mom?" Simone tapped her on the shoulder. "Don't worry. They checked our pipes, too. We're fine."

Nell lifted her head slowly. "Someone came while Miss Mildred was away? And you let them in?"

Simone panicked. "But they said they knew you! They live in 7C downstairs."

"And we got to play with Caleb!" Kenny squealed. He did jumping jacks in the middle of the living room.

"Kenneth Raymond," Nell hissed. "Stop that. Who's Caleb? What are you talking about?"

"Their son," Simone told her. "He likes to swim. Remember? We met him on the playground."

The kids' attention returned to their cartoon. Nell's hands began to tremble.

Carl, Helena . . . and Caleb. Why would they tell her they had no children? How could they have been on the train at the same time her kids were seeing them here at the apartment? The puzzle almost made her brain snap.

Nell felt her still-damp hair stick to her neck and cheeks.

Legos scattered all over the floor again, stains on countertops, across their shirts. The sink was full of dishes that reeked of sweet and sour grease.

Nell stood and shuttered the window blinds. She locked the front door.

"Please pick up your toys—all these toys on the floor." Nell could feel her voice rising. "And don't open this door until I come out of the bathroom! Do you hear me? Don't do anything!"

Simone and Kenny cowered and shook their heads yes.

Nell raised a hand to her wet hair. "Mommy just needs a shower." She repeated "I'll be fine" all the way to the bathroom.

Hot steam spilled out of the top of the glass door. She waited until the mirror fogged over and swallowed every curve of her body. She stared into the sink, its porcelain curves sweating, but saw and heard nothing this time.

In the shower, as the water beat down, Nell stared into the drain. Little bubbles percolated from within it. If she could just see through the pipes to the floor below, see what was happening in 7C. Nell pulled at her hair. A chunk of it fell, escaped her hands, and swirled around the drain. No wonder it was clogged, she thought. She bent down to pick up her hair.

Then a little swirl of red mixed into the hair. Nell rose and stepped back. The water grew darker and darker, eclipsing with the stain and stench of blood. It ran over Nell's shoulders, onto her knees and over her body, into the standing pool at the drain. As Nell turned to glance up at the showerhead, something skittered across her toes. Through the drain, tiny fingers reached up and unearthed the drain cover.

"Help us! Help!" the tiny voices cried out from within the drain.

Nell screamed and pushed the glass door so hard it collided with the wall and shattered.

From one of the ceiling vents, Nell heard more voices and the sound of dogs barking. She crept over the bathmat and past the toilet, trying not to step in the glass. The sink gurgled and overflowed with blood, from the counter onto the floor.

Nell ran to the living room and found it empty. Simone and Kenny no longer stared at the television.

"Help!" The piercing scream followed. It bounced off the living room walls.

Nell stood, stark naked and dripping blood onto the living room carpet. She noticed a note on the coffee table. She rushed over, covering her breasts with her hands.

Went to play xoxo, the note read. It was written in crayon. But the writing wasn't Kenny's, who couldn't write, or Simone's, who still scribbled her A, B, Cs. She didn't recognize the writing, its perfectly curved "p" or the way the x's and o's crowded each other.

"Help!" the scream of a child floated up from under the front door.

Nell grabbed a blanket from the couch, barely covering herself, and bolted into the hallway. She ran a few apartments down the hall and pressed her ear against Mildred's door, but there was nothing. Even after she beat against the door, no one opened it.

The cries for help echoed at the end of the hall, by the stairs. Nell followed it, slowly descending the steps, leaving bloody footprints in her wake.

As she entered the seventh floor, the screams faded and were replaced by the distraught, inconsolable cries of children. So many children. Nell's ears rang with them. She fell to her knees.

There's still time, Nell, she heard Carl's voice whisper.

"My babies. My babies," Nell whimpered. She crawled on her hands and knees toward the middle of the hall, to a door with a cross dangling from it.

Then she stood. The door to 7C was ajar, as if waiting for her. Nell wrapped her wet, bloody fingers around the knob and pushed it open.

Dirt

A thick, yellow fog swept across the city as if the face of downtown had been smeared with mud. Sofie stared at a disappearing sunset and her amber reflection in their apartment's floor-to-ceiling windows. The edges of her blonde hair were crisp from being styled that morning, and her skin looked illuminated.

In the distance, construction cranes perched like birds, and she wondered if the falling women would visit her dreams again tonight. Every night for weeks and one by one, they climbed to the tops of the cranes and plunged off. Each face turned toward her as the wind lifted their long hair. Their hands and feet floated upward, as if pulled by marionette strings. Then always, just before their bodies hit the ground, she'd wake up.

Last night, the falling woman wore a red dress, and her hair was different than the others. Shorter. A messy, crimped bob with fringe cut a full inch above her arched eyebrows. Her hair faded from brown roots to platinum blonde tips, and her eyes were hollowed and sunken. The skin beneath those eyes were so dark they appeared bruised. Still, Sofie felt she was beautiful.

Just before the woman in the red dress fell, she smiled at Sofie. The smile captured her, and she couldn't avert her gaze as the woman dove hundreds of feet into a pile of earth. When Sofie woke, she swore she, too, felt her lungs collapse and the dirt bury her body.

Sofie shuddered at the memory. She didn't want to blame the city, but she couldn't help it. Ever since they'd moved to the South, she'd had nightmares fueled by the city's jaundiced skin. Their apartment was on the edge of the historic district, wrought with graffiti and cries in the middle of the night. The abandoned railroad tracks below them echoed of creaking bones. She smelled a persistent, pungent odor of a rain that never came. Every time she was about to step outside, she caught her breath.

Yet she couldn't decide which was worse—the dead air of the city or having to look at it every day from the museum-perfect brightness of their home. The apartment's interior was grandiose, like her husband Grant. Dark marble countertops woven with real gold, handstitched chenille pillows decorating milky white leather couches, and a fireplace in a city too warm to ever see autumn. A maid came every few days to ensure the apartment's spotlessness, leaving Sofie with anxiety until the next visit. If anything was out of place, Grant could sense it immediately.

Grant was rarely home from his job in finance, but when he was, he fixated on Sofie. He had a fetish about her hands that was attractive at first, with him always wanting to caress and hold them in public. But once a ring was on her finger, his obsession flourished into control. Her nails, her hair, her skin all needed to meet his approval. She was the living doll in his dollhouse.

Sofie gazed across the city, where the cranes, only a couple blocks away, swayed gracefully back and forth in their routines, then she glanced down. Two washers swung by on their bosun's chairs a few floor below. They trapped the atmospheric stains and smudges against the glass with their squeegees, then dragged them back down into the city streets near Jesser House, the historic building on the corner that had always attracted her attention. Once a dormitory for female travelers, Jesser House had been crushed between the hands of time. It ached with dislocated window frames and siding like cracked ribs. When the honeyed fog grew dense, it stuck fingers into the guts of the dilapidated house and left tawny smears along the exterior.

As she watched, a pale shimmer darted within one of the broken windows of Jesser House. Sofie squinted until whispers of blonde hair materialized, framing a soft, oval jawline. The woman's cheeks were covered with filth, but Sofie recognized her. The red sweetheart neckline of her dress and thick, chocolate bangs matted to her forehead gave her away. Slowly, as if the woman realized she was being watched, her eyes drifted upward. When she spotted Sofie in her picture window, the woman exposed a row of rotting teeth in a smile. Then she cocked her head and withdrew into the collapsing estate again.

Sofie's heart raced. Had she seen this homeless woman on the streets before? Is that how the woman had made it into her dreams? She recognized the transients who circulated the historic district by day and nestled in its cavities at night. From her birds-eye view she watched their blurred figures beg for food or money, huddle for safety, and vanish into the lusterless amber mist. She was once one, too, when she lived in the North. Before Grant. Before this city. Sometimes she felt like a foreigner in her own life because of it.

She disrobed from her silk nightgown and slipped into her day dress. In the refrigerator sat leftovers Grant had rejected the previous night, something Sofie had delivered but couldn't finish on her own.

"Leftovers are for the trash," Grant would always say whenever she asked for a bag after a lavish meal.

"But it's such waste," she'd insist.

"Which is why it goes in the waste. Get it? You act like you don't know where your next meal is coming from. Stop trying to embarrass me." Then he'd wave the waiter away.

She plucked the box of leftovers from the middle shelf and sucked on the tips of two cold-but-fragrant garlic French fries as she headed down to the first floor. Just past the front doors, the tarnished faces of the historic buildings came into view. As she crossed the street, a woman with expensive, pungent perfume walked past, and Sofie covered her nose with one hand.

Even though it was the middle of the day, the corner was practically abandoned. Shadows of the eastward cranes stretched into the abandoned lots and along the empty streets. The only sound was a man a few blocks away, pacing between two light posts and shouting "Fuck you!" repeatedly at what must have been a ghost.

As she approached Jesser House, Sofie felt eyes at her heels, crawling up the bare skin of her calves. She stopped where the fragmented curb met the concrete walkway. A faded sign still hung on Jesser House's front door. But no one was there in the crooked frames, underneath the tilted porch columns, or in between the tooth-like bars of the stairway banister. Every blade of grass had shrunk and withered into soot years ago, leaving a wet residue clinging to the bottom of the house. The rest of the yard was parched.

In the dirt beside the walkway, Sofie noticed handprints. Their shallow impressions meandered from the house to the corner then up onto the sidewalk. No footprints accompanied them. She bent to examine them closer when a hand grasped her shoulder. She turned to find the babbling homeless man beside her, and she screamed. His eyes widened as she dropped the leftovers and ran.

Her heart thumped in her chest all the way up the elevator. She fumbled with the door lock to get inside, only to find her hands were covered in dusty grime. She wondered if, in a daze, she'd fallen while fleeing from the strange man. By the time she'd washed her hands in the kitchen and stepped onto the balcony again, the man, leftovers, and trail of smudged handprints were all gone. She gazed in disbelief as the fog churned into the shapes of skirt hems and tendrils of hair with its saffron brushstrokes.

For the rest of the afternoon, she stayed locked in the bathroom, with no view of the city. When Grant arrived, he asked her if she'd been outside, then started complaining about the mess someone had left on their front door handle.

He stopped when he saw her. "Jesus, Sofie. Your hands are filthy. I scheduled a manicure for you today. Did you forget?"

She'd forgotten. She picked at the dirt beneath her nails, then hid both of her hands behind her back.

Grant furrowed his brows. "You know the importance of tomorrow night's dinner for my boss—and my career. I want you to look beautiful, to be the most beautiful woman there," he insisted. Then he scowled. "Not like how I found you, living out of your car. I'll reschedule your manicure for tomorrow."

Sofie sauntered toward the big picture windows and the twilight cityscape. The tips of each crane were marked with glowing red lights. "Grant, do you know why this city always smells like ... decay?" She lifted a fingernail to her mouth and tasted the grit with her tongue.

Grant undid his tie. "Clean cities have no people. If you insist, I can hire a driver to take you somewhere."

"That's not what I meant," she moaned. "It's this fog. Don't you think it's strange? Such a dreadful color, and it never goes away."

"It's just congestion from all the cars," he said. "The heat aggravates it."

Sofie wondered how this could be true when the historic district roads were relatively empty.

"I think I'm sick," she mumbled.

"Then take an antacid. You're going to dinner tomorrow, and you're going to be perfect."

* * *

Grant was already at work by the time the maid began vacuuming, but he left Sofie a note with the time and address of her appointment. The salon was only a few blocks north, and when she arrived, a young nail tech with a dusting of freckles across her cheeks greeted her. She informed Sofie that her husband had already paid for and chosen the color.

"Golden leaf. To go with your outfit for the party," the nail tech explained. She held up the iridescent bottle of varnish.

Something told Sofie that bribing the young woman for a different color wouldn't work. The woman beamed as if she longed for a husband like Grant, who pampered her and bought her gifts. If only she knew.

Sofie winced as the young woman buried her soft pink nails under layers of the flaxen lacquer. Nestled between the sparkles was the color of old bruises and rot. She could practically smell the stench, and it made her want to vomit.

As the woman hummed to herself, Sofie closed her eyes and slowed her breathing. An image of the nail tech flashed through her mind. Her long black hair was freed from the tight bun at the nape of her neck, and her beautifully manicured hands and feet floated through the air. She wore a white lace dress, paler than her skin. Dangling above her was a downtown crane.

Sofie gasped and opened her eyes, then lunged toward the nail tech. "Have we met before?" Her voice was desperate and high-pitched. The nail tech jumped, dropping the polish, and they watched it roll off the edge of the table and spill across the floor.

The nail tech stood and spoke hurried Chinese to an older man, who trotted over with a mop. "I'll get another, then we'll do your feet," she told Sofie. They spent the rest of the hour in silence.

On the walk home, Sofie felt the weight of the polish on her hands, smelling like rotten eggs no matter how hard she scrubbed them in the salon bathroom. It was all she could do to not pick it off from disgust. But it would be no use. The nail tech assured her the polish would last for two weeks.

The pale bisque glow of the streetlights illuminated before her and cut through the smog as she navigated back to the apartment complex. Jesser House came into view, and despite the heat, Sofie felt a chill touch her skin. She scurried toward home, her eyes down. She didn't want to see the dingy grin of the woman in Jesser House's window again.

At the corner, the same handprints she saw the previous day on the sidewalk appeared beneath her feet. The palms were heavy and cracked through the center, with delicate fingers nearly severed at each base. She followed their trail toward her apartment complex's entrance, where the hands climbed along the concrete wall and over a balcony. About eight stories up, Sofie noticed a red skirt fluttering through the mist.

She rushed into her building and the elevator. On the eighth floor, she knocked on several doors, but no one answered. By the time she returned to her own unit, Grant was waiting in the living room, dressed in his tux, sipping on two brown fingers of scotch. She darted past him and unlatched one of the windows then stepped onto the balcony. The railing cut into her hips as she peered down, trying to find the woman in red. Every balcony below was empty except for some furniture and potted plants.

Grant grabbed her by the wrist and pulled her back inside. "What's the meaning of this? You're an absolute wreck, and the driver will be here in half an hour!"

The disdain on his face left her fumbling for words. "Did you see her?" She pointed toward the balcony. "I swear I saw—"

His grip tightened around her sparkling fingertips, then his voice lowered. "I can't believe you'd embarrass me like this, after all I've done for you, Sofie. You were nothing when I found you. Now you have everything at your fingertips. So get in the shower, then put on the dress I bought for you. I will not let you sabotage my promotion!"

Sofie slunk toward the bathroom, where the golden dress lay across the chaise. Swaths of beige fabric plunged in a V shape down to the waist then ballooned out in thick layers. The odor of the fabric made her turn and vomit in the sink.

When she lifted her face, she finally saw in the mirror what Grant had seen. Streaks of brown ran from her hairline to her chin. Her mascara was smeared, and her matted hair fell limp around her face. When she touched her cheek, the backs of her hands were stained with sediment that covered the fresh nail polish.

She scrubbed in the shower until her skin flushed and the water turned clear. She could hear Grant cursing about keeping the driver waiting while she donned the golden dress and finished her makeup.

Grant dragged her from the car to his boss's townhome, keeping a tight grip, but he released her the moment a colleague approached and offered him a glass of scotch. Sofie was left to stare at the mahogany finishes and opaque curtains draped like dreary lashes over double hung windows. She waded through the women in their opulent dresses of velvet, silk, and sequins, searching for a familiar face.

Two drinks in, she recognized all of them. Their dresses first, then their dark and puffy eyes, their dull skin and sunken cheeks. They floated between the men and each other like ghosts. Their lips moved, but none of them mouthed a word. When Sofie retreated to the bathroom, she felt the entire room pause to watch her leave.

She coughed up dirt in the sink, spitting brown flecks into the white porcelain. Grit lined her gums and stuck between her teeth. It covered the palms of her hands. Each time she swallowed she tasted it—the flavor of that rancid yellow fog. She felt it ferment in her guts and simmer at her fingertips.

"I feel sick. I have to go home," she found herself whispering into Grant's ear.

His appalled glance down at her confirmed that she was unwell. He hailed a cab, and when it parked in front of their apartment complex, she felt some relief. There were no handprints along the sidewalk or scaling the building, no skirt hem dangling from above.

The elevator crawled up to their floor and chimed as the door opened. Sofie made her way through the dark apartment to the bed and fell into a deep-yet-dreamless slumber instantly. When she woke just before 2 a.m., a sound like tree branches scraping along the bedroom windowpane echoed. But she knew there were no trees. After stretching out a hand, she realized Grant hadn't returned from the party yet either. She lifted herself onto her elbows then swung around until she felt her toes touch the floorboards.

Groggy and disoriented, she fumbled for the light switch in the hallway. When her vision cleared, she recognized a palm print on the couch armrest, as dark and muddy as the leather was white. Soil had dribbled down the side and onto the floor. Sofie followed trails of handprints as they tracked across each living room wall and up their length to the ceiling. They covered the ceiling, too.

She remembered her own dirty hands and aligned them with the prints on the wall. A perfect, delicate match of browned fingers, one covering the other.

The dense, mustard-colored fog outside pressed against the glass. Sofie released the latch and drew the screen, letting the mist pour inside. She could only see as far as the balcony railing, so she reached out and gripped the banister. More handprints stamped the platform and ascended to the balcony above. She squinted upward through the haze, searching for the hem of a red dress or a soiled grin.

Then she felt two hands thrust her from behind, as she fell from the balcony into the belly of the fog.

* * *

When Sofie woke, it was still dark, but an unfamiliar light

cascaded over her. Moonlight, she realized. But it was no dream. No mattress. No apartment. Up above, the cranes hovered. She sat propped up against the chassis of one.

She blinked through the dust at the dirt trenches and piles of construction materials left for the next morning. In a shard of glass beside her, she saw her reflection. The swath of fabric along her right shoulder was ripped, her hair rumpled. Her teeth felt like powder, and she drew back her lips to find mud caked over the enamel. The golden veneer on her fingernails was covered in the same.

She latched onto the chassis and pulled herself up then pulled higher, until she scaled the crane, until she escaped the putrid fog of the city and reached the precipice. Below her, the façade of every building came into view. She recognized Jesser House, the train tracks, the corner where hands prints lined the sidewalk, the front door of her apartment complex.

She thought of Grant and his precious promotion, and the cringing expressions directed at her during the party. He'd have some explaining to do tonight, but not just for her. He'd lose his temper, and without her there to take the brunt of it, he'd say something, do something awful to someone else. He'd put a stain on his own reputation, because they'd see when the shiny veneer started to peel back that he was nothing but dirt. Just like her.

And the women of the city, who passed by on the dimly lit streets below her, dangling their couture purses, flashing their made-up faces, strolling along in their opulent skirts and heels, they didn't even suspect she was up there. Watching them. Knowing them too well. They were dolls in dollhouses, too, and she wanted to shake them for it, to fuss their hair, dirty their homes, muddy their dreams.

So she rose to her feet and shuffled to the edge of the crane, feeling the wind lift the tips of her hair. She would make them finally see her. She would wake them up.

As she fell forward, her skirt began to float, and a smile swept across her face.

The Lovebugs

After a summer of record-setting heat, Carissa longed for the day when she could ride her bicycle to work again. She stood in her red, sweat-stained uniform under the overhang of Prime Foods and squinted across the parking lot in search of her fiancé's truck. He'd offered to pick up her bike at the repair shop and swing by at the end of her shift. She loved how he remembered the name of her bike, Pearl, dubbed for its milky white frame and saddle, and that he treated it with as much devotion as a man his age would a hot rod. He loved it just because she loved it.

Her cell phone buzzed in her purse: *I need to see u. Can I come over tonight?*

Carissa rolled her eyes. Brad. She'd blocked his number a dozen times since they broke up two years ago. But he always demanded her attention as soon as she thought herself free.

Cars at the edge of the parking lot seemed to float along in phantom pools, reflective mirages of sky that cut apart the pavement, as if Prime Foods was nestled along the Florida shoreline and a slow, crawling tide was about to come in.

Darius's truck emerged from that tide as Carissa slid the phone back into her purse. She waved as he pulled up beside her.

The truck looked covered in fleas, but it was the lovebugs. Hundreds of tiny, black, two-by-two bodies smashed against the grill, with their dull, yellow guts streaked across the truck's shiny paint. Carissa peered into the back. Pearl had been stowed away from the threat of the lovebugs, her pristine white coat still as fresh as fallen snow.

Carissa opened the door and climbed into the chassis beside Darius.

"I'm gonna need to wash her down again when we get home," Darius told her. "Doesn't matter which road I choose. They're everywhere."

Carissa nodded. "It's May. Lovebug season in Florida. Sorry, babe. I should have warned you."

Darius cupped her hand in his and pulled the truck out of the parking lot and onto the road.

He'd uprooted his life in Oklahoma after they were engaged in the spring, moving to the Lake Okeechobee house Carissa inherited from her grandmother. It was the first time any man had moved anywhere for Carissa. This and Darius's calm in the face of summer threats new to him—heatwaves, hurricanes, and lovebugs—meant he must truly be the one.

Carissa let this thought ease her mind as the air conditioning cooled her skin and blew her worries about Brad's message into their rear view. She freed her ponytail and erased her lipstick in the mirror with a napkin, then unpinned the name badge from her chest.

"Better," she sighed.

The Florida sunshine glimmered against her engagement ring. A small but proud round diamond, with a gold band.

"Still like it?" Darius asked, noticing her noticing the ring.

"I love it," she said. "And the man who gave it to me, of

course."

"Must be an awesome guy," he teased.

They switched the radio to a local news station, where the hosts talked about the fishing forecast, the enduring presence of mosquitoes, and the return of the lovebugs.

"You know," he said, "I heard from some guy at the gas station that those things were created at the University of Florida. Said it was a botched experiment, trying to create sterile females to mate with the male mosquitoes."

Carissa chuckled. "That's not true. I don't know why people still believe that."

"Can't really be sure, though. Can we?" asked Darius. "Only the bugs know the truth."

She was sure.

She glanced out her window at the brown-baked yards passing beside them. Deteriorating trailers. Roadkill. Weeds. She could be sure, because Brad had worked as an entomologist with the University of Florida before he was fired and forced to take a part-time job as a cashier at Prime Foods. When she'd met his friends, former colleagues, they'd assured her the lovebugs weren't an invention of the faculty.

Carissa couldn't tell Darius this. For him, Brad didn't exist, and she liked it that way. If Brad didn't exist, then all the things he'd done to hurt her didn't exist either. How, in front of customers, he once told her if she ever left, he'd kill them both. How, after he was fired from Prime Foods and they broke up, he kept trying to intercept her at her car at the end of her shift. How she still occasionally found voice messages left by an unfamiliar number, with Brad's breath reverberating in her ear.

Within the first year apart, she was certain he'd planted a

scorpion in her mailbox and a black widow spider on the bike rack outside of Prime Foods, right next to Pearl's lock. She slowly began to learn that whenever something felt out of place, Brad was nearby.

When Darius offered to move in with her, she was relieved. No creatures except the usual Florida pests had appeared since he'd moved in.

As they pulled into the driveway, Carissa felt phone vibrations in her purse again. She slipped a hand into the folds to mute it.

The truck braked in the middle of the drive instead of pulling up to the garage. "What the hell?" Darius said, peering past her and out the window.

Scattered beside their front door and the small staircase leading to it were the remains of the house number tiles, once cemented to the concrete block exterior. Whatever removed it had also sheared the colonial blue paint off the side of the house.

They got out of the truck and paced around the front entrance. Carissa noticed a gas can was resting on top of the bushes against the house, spout down and emptied. Darius smelled it first. He quickly covered his mouth and nose, then she smelled it, too.

"Someone seriously poured gas on the bushes all around your grandma's house?" he muttered through his fingers. "What did they think they were going to do—light concrete blocks on fire?"

At the end of the block, tires squealed, and a car bolted from down the road. She felt a lump fill her throat as the car sped out of sight.

Darius turned to her. "All these plants are going to die now. I'm sorry, hun."

She shook her head and told him she wanted to go inside. They climbed back into the truck and closed the garage door behind them.

Darius unloaded her bike while she excused herself to the bathroom. The minute she closed the bathroom door, she pulled out her phone.

Brad texted: *I got u some new lights for ur bike.*

Why aren't u responding? What are u hiding?

Do u think u can get rid of me that easy?

U never appreciated me. Just text back.

And so on. She pieced together a plot suited to Brad. At the height of his anger, he must have driven to her house and vandalized the house number and poured the gasoline. She wondered if he knew about Darius and the engagement, wondered how many times he had driven by the house since Darius had moved in.

The summer afternoon rains poured all the way into the night. She told Darius the thunder put her on edge when he asked why she kept checking her phone. But even after the thunder stopped, she jumped each time a twig snapped or an animal cried through the darkness outside. Carissa didn't know what to expect next. Brad tapping a finger against her window? Him showing up at her doorstep with a match?

Darius hugged her tight as they snuggled into bed. He was usually snoring before she finished brushing her teeth. "The vandalism got you shook up, sweetie? Everything okay?"

She shook her head yes and watched him turn out the light. As the snoring began, Carissa stared wide-eyed through the bedroom window, through sheets of rain, waiting for the shadow of Brad to materialize.

* * *

Carissa woke the next morning to an empty bed, the smell of coffee, and a note from Darius beside the coffee pot: *Went to work early, then the farmer's market to get that honey you like. Cooler this morning after the rain. Perfect for a bike ride. I'll pick you and Pearl up if you girls need it.*

She retrieved her helmet from a pile in the corner of the garage and set it on the table beside her coffee. But a stench that seemed to seep through the kitchen windows killed her appetite. After dressing into her uniform, she stepped outside. The putrid gas smell from last night persisted, in spite of the rain. Death marked the hedges and flower beds, curled and browned as if the summer heat had wilted them. She covered her nose with both her hands and walked back inside.

Darius was right about the morning ride. With overcast clouds blocking the sun and the dew of last night's rain still cooling every surface, Carissa rode Pearl the fifteen minutes to work without breaking a sweat. But by the middle of the day, the story had changed. Heat simmered on the ground and threatened to suffocate every living thing as it clawed its way up. A blanket of gray still covered the sky.

Just as Carissa clocked out for lunch, Darius texted her: *Check the news if you can.* She greeted a few coworkers in the break room and found them surrounding the one small television in the corner. The farmer's market was in the middle of the screen. White tents in narrow rows covered in millions of black specks. The lovebugs fluttered across the screen as if the cameraman had walked into a swarm of bees. One or two people rushed between the tents and tried to take video footage with their phones, hands waving and arms smacking in front of their faces.

Every piece of jewelry, jar of honey, framed photo, and trash can was dotted with lovebugs.

The footage ended when a blurry oval body entered the edge of the screen, followed by another and another, until the screen went black.

Her phone buzzed again: *Got your honey. But they're shutting down the market and half of downtown until this stops.*

The news report switched to a story about a driver who lost control of his car along the highway. Lovebugs were to blame. Witnesses said they struggled to see the road after the swarm descended.

Are you home yet? Carissa texted back. *They're causing accidents.*

She finished a last, nervous bite of her sandwich when Darius texted back: *Safe at home.*

Carissa breathed a sigh of relief.

For the rest of her shift, the lovebug infestation was the talk of every grocery shopper. One manager let the staff know that toilet paper and eggs were being purchased in large quantities. If she was low at home, she needed to grab some now. But her grandmother, raised during the Depression, had enough storage space built into the house that Carissa felt obligated to keep the shelves stocked.

Then the manager ordered them to close the store. The swarm was headed to their part of town, and it might be dangerous for them to drive home if they waited much longer.

Carissa texted Darius that she was on her way. He offered to come pick her up, but she insisted on biking. The last thing she wanted was an injured or stranded fiancé because of the swarm, and she knew the route better than him.

She clipped on her helmet and popped up the kickstand, only

to hear another text ding on her phone: *This has gone on long enough. I can't live without u. I'm at the edge of the parking lot. Plz come talk.*

Carissa crouched down and rolled her bike backward into the shadow of the Prime Foods overhang. She imagined him circling his parked vehicle like a buzzard killing time. When the sliding doors reopened, she slid back inside the store. She waved to her manager on her way toward the back exit, but he was preoccupied with wrapping up deli meats.

She rounded the building and pedaled toward the side road, picking up her pace. A cloud of black loomed along the horizon behind her, ready to overtake the shadowy sky.

Small batches of lovebugs already floated through the path back home. Carissa knew they didn't bite or sting. But the sheer number of them smothering full-stop traffic along the road and forcing people to abandon their cars frightened her. She witnessed one man, his figure overtaken by an animated swarm, drop to his knees and fight against them.

Carissa switched gears and peddled through the cloud of bugs as fast as Pearl and her legs would let her.

At the house, only a few pests littered the mailbox and driveway concrete. Darius had left the garage door open for her. Once inside, she ran for the switch to close it. She was breathless by the time she reached the living room, where Darius sat, transfixed by the television.

"They nearly got a news reporter," he said, not even turning toward her. "Covered his neck and started crawling in his mouth, until someone pulled him inside the news van."

Carissa gulped. She couldn't tell Darius she saw a man nearly buried in lovebugs back on the highway.

He turned to Carissa then, his eyes framed by tired wrinkles and his brow furrowed in worry. "They said we aren't allowed to leave our homes. Is this normal?"

Carissa shook her head and eased onto the couch beside him.

When the news went to a commercial break, she slipped into the bathroom and changed out of her work clothes. Sweat stains lined the middle of the back and formed a ring around the collar. The pale smell of gasoline had latched onto the wet fabric. Carissa pressed the shirt against her nostrils and almost gagged.

When she glanced down at her phone, she saw more texts from Brad.

I know u still love me. Why'd u leave? I come to rescue u from the lovebugs, and this is what I get?

Another lump caught in her throat. She remembered the myth about the lovebugs' origin and his time at the University of Florida, how he was fired for some undisclosed problem—and, in retrospect, she had just assumed it was stalking another ex.

She messaged him: *Did you have something to do with this?*

The ellipsis on the screen indicated he was responding for several minutes. Then it stopped. *Maybe. Maybe not.*

She threw the phone onto the floor, then cupped her face in her hands. If she told Darius everything about Brad now, she didn't know how he would react.

"You okay?" Darius breathed through the bathroom door. "Been in there a while."

"I'll be out in a minute," she said. She could practically taste the gasoline in her mouth.

The infestation grew throughout the afternoon. More reports of fleeing, more accidents, even a witness who claimed to see the bugs kill someone. Carissa and Darius made dinner for themselves but couldn't finish.

Outside, against the windows facing the street, they noticed the dull black flecks gathering. A random film across the glass at first. Then they overflowed the gutters above, until one of the frailer connectors collapsed. Water and leaves crashed onto the lawn. The lovebugs covered that, too.

Carissa remembered what Brad said about lovebugs one summer when they were still together, why the bugs thrived in southern states like Florida. The dampness and decaying plant matter made for a perfect meal. This was also why they congregated along the highways, where the smell of gasoline exhaust mimicked the smell of decay.

Gasoline. Carissa leaned her head against the windowpane of the living room. Below, every bush butting up against the house was covered, abuzz with double heads and legs stepping over each other. She glanced across the street to find her neighbor's front door and windows covered as well. All that remained of their mailbox, shaped like a dolphin, was its silhouette. Even the ground below it pooled with lovebugs.

A car crept into view and inched into her neighbor's driveway, spewing a trail of exhaust behind it. The red brake lights beamed through the hail of lovebugs, then flashed off into park. But after a few more moments, she watched the car navigate a turnaround and park once again at the end of the drive, facing her property this time.

The insects whirred around the car, sank onto the hood, and sacrificed their bellies to the brightness and warmth of the headlights. The driver cut the engine.

Carissa waited for one of her neighbors to evacuate the vehicle, to run, hands waving through the air. She waited for them to keep their mouths and eyes shielded from the storm of bugs. But no one appeared.

She squinted, and through the sea of legs and wings, she caught a glimpse of the man seated at the wheel. Dark eyes behind thick, rectangular glasses. A slim beard along his chin. Brad.

She gasped and hid beneath the window frame. Darius immediately ran to her side.

He placed his palm against her back. "The gas smell got you sick? Just stay back from the window. Over here."

He started standing, but Carissa grabbed him by the collar, pulling him down on top of her.

"Don't. Just don't look out there," she whispered. "Please. Help me close all the window blinds."

Darius was confused, but he helped her crawl along the living room carpet and grasp the plastic knobs at the end of each cord to pull the blinds shut.

The room went dark except for the glow of the television screen. Darius stood again. But Carissa remained on the floor, her hands visibly shaking. Every time the engagement ring caught the light of the screen, it seemed to flash an SOS.

Darius recognized her fear and bent down again, hugging her until the shaking slowed. "He's here," she whispered through her tears. "He's here."

"Who?"

"My ex."

Darius released her from his embrace. "Outside? In this? But why?"

She freed every detail of the past in breathless sentences—the texts, the threats, the stalking. How Brad felt she owed him another chance and wouldn't stop until she gave it to him. How he may have something to do with the lovebugs.

"At the very least, Brad knew they were coming," she told

him. "He wasn't trying to burn down the house yesterday. He was trying to kill all our plants. The lovebugs are attracted to the smell of gas and decay."

Darius remained calm. "Do you think we can still make a run for it? The news said it's not happening anywhere but Okeechobee."

She shook her head. "You saw the reports. It's too dangerous. We shouldn't leave the house."

Darius nodded, but as he turned toward the windows again, his lower jaw clenched. "Think it's at least safe enough to go out there and rip your ex's head off?"

"I'm hoping, now that he can't see us, he'll go away."

They turned their attention back to the house, devising ways to fortify it from the lovebugs. They were small enough to wiggle into the crawl space beneath or attic above, but she doubted they could get through the vents.

"They could also cut off the air conditioning unit outside. But they'd have to—"

As the last word fell from her mouth, a loud sputter rang from outside. The air handler hiccupped and died.

"Shit," Carissa hissed.

Two taps sounded at their front door. They both jumped, then Darius put a finger to his lips. She tiptoed to the window again and made a narrow slit between the blinds. A figure dressed in white stood on the front porch steps. At first it looked like an astronaut. But as Carissa blinked, the helmet morphed into a mesh veil with zippers securing it to the neck. A beekeeper's suit. Flocks of lovebugs buzzed around and landed on the suit. But they never overwhelmed it.

The figure knocked on the door again, more insistent this time. Through the mesh she saw the beard and glasses.

"It's him. Oh, God," she said, stepping back. "He's at the front door. Why can't he just leave me alone?"

Darius rolled up his sleeves and grabbed the door handle.

"No!" she screamed.

"Lock this door behind me—and don't open it again until I've beat the shit out of him. Understand?"

Carissa didn't have time to respond. Darius bolted onto the porch. Then the door slammed shut behind him, and she lunged forward to twist the deadbolt. Some lovebugs infiltrated in the commotion. They fluttered around her face and landed on the walls. She reached for the fly swatter and struck every pair she could find.

Outside, the sound of shouts and fists pounding echoed. Someone slammed into the door with such force, she thought it might break open. Then everything quieted to the dull rhythm of the lovebugs beating against the house.

"Darius?" she said, her cheek pressed against the door. "Darius?"

She scurried to the window and looked through the blinds. Someone lay crumpled at the bottom of the stairs, covered in bugs, a tar-like mound. Carissa couldn't even make out the color of his hair, the shade of his eyes, his shape.

Then something moved in her peripheral vision, just in front of the door. The beekeeper's suit raised its hand and knocked twice more.

She covered her mouth in horror. The black mound was Darius. Lovebugs, drilling into his ear canals. Lovebugs, covering his eyes until he couldn't see to strike. Lovebugs, crawling into his mouth and nose until they cornered him into his last breath. She wanted to tear through the door and cover his body with her own.

Her head spun. She closed her eyes and pressed her shoulder against the wall, where the smell of gas threatened to take her own breath away. "Darius," she cried out, and when silence answered, she screamed louder. "Darius!"

Carissa didn't know when Brad returned to his car, when the sun set, when she stopped screaming. But her voice, hoarse and raw, eventually gave up and left the shell of her body behind. The summer heat trapped inside the house matted her hair against her scalp. Another shirt soaked. But this time, she couldn't tell if it was sweat or tears.

It was hard to sleep that night, between the heat and the thoughts throbbing inside her head. What if she kept her past with Brad a secret? Or what if she'd mentioned him sooner? Would Darius still be here, safe beside her? Would Brad have been scared off so long ago that the lovebugs never manifested? Either fate was preferable to this one. She could have made that choice. She should have.

At one point before dawn, her cell phone lost its signal, and the texts from Brad stopped. But he persisted. Each time she glanced out the door's peephole, she saw the car still parked in the neighbor's driveway. Every few hours, knocks came at the door, and she would cover her ears until he stopped. She lost track of time and days as the dark circles beneath her eyes grew darker. She wished for sleep only so she could wake up from this nightmare. More than anything, she shuddered at the thought of Brad stepping over Darius's body—that Darius's body was even out there.

She woke one morning to find notes plastered across the living room windows. Hearts with her and Brad's initials in thick, black, permanent marker. *You still love me. It was fate that your fiancé died. Now we can be together.* The paper pieces were like fat exclamation marks drawn across a black chalkboard. She felt the darkened walls and ceilings and floors begin to close on her. She grabbed a figurine off a nearby bookshelf just in case.

A noise came from down the hallway, closer to the bedroom. If Brad had made it into the house, she would be ready for him. She tiptoed past the couches and toward the hallway. Along the ceiling, near the opening to the attic, a dozen lovebug pairs swarmed. She batted them away with her hands and spit at any that neared her mouth. But they kept leaking out of the edges of the attic door as if it were a faucet. When the stream became too much to hold back, Carissa backed away toward the living room again.

Slowly, a pair floated past her face, one of the lovebugs awkwardly dragging the other behind it, still attached but lifeless. She remembered Brad once told her how the mating of the lovebugs ends. The male dies, but he refuses to let go. His body clings to the female until she's ready to lay eggs. Then they detach, and she dies as well.

The pair piloted their jagged and clumsy path toward the garage door and landed there. Carissa opened the door and watched as the pair spun circles in the air, then fluttered down to the black handlebars of her bike. Except for the tiny red thoraxes at each end, the pair seemed to disappear into the grip. She placed her hand beside them, and the female crawled onto Carissa's ring finger. The proud, round diamond still shone brightly through their dark bodies.

She lifted the kickstand and pressed the button to open the garage door, letting the flood of bugs enter the house. She wheeled Pearl forward carefully and sat on the saddle. Across the street was Brad in his beekeeper suit, just exiting his car again.

As Brad watched the garage door raise, his eyes widened, and the edges of his beard lifted. He jogged across the street toward the house, toward her, his arms outstretched. But the joy on his face turned to anguish as the bugs covered Carissa's legs. They climbed her torso and neck, swept their black bodies across her lips. He froze and lifted his hands to his mouth, forgetting about the suit. She smiled. Then Brad and the gasoline odor and everything disappeared.

As the lovebugs enveloped her, Carissa remembered the first morning she woke up beside Darius. That warm cocoon of his arms around her, hands tickling, buried beneath their sheets. His kisses landed on every inch of her body until her skin felt alive.

Daughters

Rue stripped off her nightgown in front of the refrigerator, then tucked an ice cube into her cheek and chewed. Beads of sweat collected along her spine. Outside, a humid summer night pressed its body against every surface of the condo and covered each window with a film of condensation. Soggy bed sheets weren't worth waking Ron in the middle of the night. She'd tried this before, and his crankiness was worse than the two of them simmering in a pool of her sweat until morning.

Rue glanced down at her naked body, grayed by the dim light of the storm. Ghostly white stretch marks materialized along her lower abdomen, while purple, threadlike veins painted spiderwebs on her outer thighs. She slid her fingers across the glass and longed to see a younger woman, then imagined herself bathing beneath the cool, persistent rain.

From across the parking lot, the pale lights of the community pool called out to her. The pool had been her salvation ever since they moved to Florida. The first year was like a permanent vacation. No more raking leaves or shoveling snow. No more weeks without sunshine. Then the change started, and Rue cursed the merciless, year-round Florida heat.

The community pool was the one spot where she felt relief.

Big fans, shady palms, a pool aerator, and eight bronzed scuppers that continuously poured refreshing water into the deep end. She licked her lips and swore she could smell chlorine through the windowpane.

Rue glanced over at her crocheted swimsuit cover-up, still lounging across an armchair after a visit to the pool earlier in the week. She slipped into the breezy fabric and knotted it around her waist. As she grabbed her keys, she heard Ron's snoring echo down the hall.

Beads of heavy rain drenched Rue's rosy-white hair as she walked along the winding community path. The outside was quiet, except for the rainfall bouncing off the thin plastic tops of golf carts, which were so popular around here. She hadn't visited the pool at this time of night before. Hours: dawn to dusk, the sign read, followed by a list of rules. But she figured no one would discover her. The only threat was the elderly front desk guardsmen, who preferred card games to security checks after midnight.

At the entrance, a handwritten sign covered the original: Pool drained. Closed for repair. Her heart sank. Still, she heard gurgling water just past the wrought iron gate. She fiddled with the latch to find it open, so she tiptoed through.

Ixora hedges with citrus-red blooms hugged two sides of the pool deck. Hundreds of droplets clung like clear cocoons from the bars of the perimeter fence. The pool was barely partitioned from the rest of the deck by yellow "caution" tape, strung between traffic cones and tall poles lodged in buckets of cement. The pool hadn't been drained, though, as the sign warned.

It was full, and soft red lights pulsed from within. She'd never seen it lit before. The high, semicircular wall of scuppers at the other end also circulated the hue—eight rich, red appendages baptizing the deep end.

All but a few lounge chairs were piled beneath the cabanas. So Rue disrobed and eased her naked body onto the steps at the shallow end of the pool. The ripples distorted her image. One ankle narrowed to almost nothing, while the sole of the other foot ballooned under the water. The broken blood vessels became animated, like spiders crawling up her calves.

She sank down to her chin and let her feet rise. The feeling of floating, of being wrapped in something cooler than her skin, finally relaxed her. Her breathing slowed, and her eyes shut as the rain fizzled out, barely tapping against her forehead.

When she opened her eyes again, she saw a fat spider poised a few feet away on one of the tiles. It stepped onto the surface of the water with such grace that Rue was mesmerized. Instead of sinking, it drifted and hugged its body in tight except for two of the front legs. Those legs curled up and forward, until its silhouette resembled a black swan.

Rue swam toward the deep end of the pool so as not to disturb the spider. Each spout at the far wall spilled like arteries left to drain. She thought of her spider veins and how they'd appeared just a few years ago during her pregnancy. Then the memory of her miscarriage rushed forward with a jolt. The bright red blood as it billowed along the front of her nightgown. A scream she could still feel in her throat. The pain had rippled outward, from her abdomen to her toes. Then it was over. She woke up in a hospital bed next to Ron and the unfortunate news. How could something so small, in time and space, cause so much pain? It had marked her body—the rest of her life—and in the end she got nothing for it.

She never believed they had time for a child until one slipped into existence. Ron had mapped out a carefully calibrated path toward early retirement in Florida ever since they married. Then a child came, unexpected and accidental, and she prepared a world for it. That little face on the ultrasound haunted her dreams. She'd always wanted a daughter.

So without telling Ron, she chased another chance, scheduling appointments with one doctor, then another. They balked at her age or encouraged adoption. Then the last one performed a hormone test and counted the follicles left in her ovaries. She was on the cusp of menopause. Her egg stores were depleted. No convincing was needed. At her age, she was more likely to have a heart attack than to conceive. And if she did conceive and hemorrhaged again, it could mean losing both of their lives.

Rue felt a trickle against her cheek and wiped away the tear with the back of her hand—a hand marked with a starburst of purple veins just below her thin skin. It throbbed with the memory. Throughout her limbs, the rest of her broken veins burned in unison.

Rue buried the hand in the maroon waters of the pool then paddled toward the spouts gushing from the high wall. She slipped her crown beneath one. Lush fingertips rapped against her head, and a shiver ran down her spine. She closed her eyes. The fever was about to break. She could almost taste it.

Then the water hardened to tickling pinpricks that crawled along her scalp and shoulders. She opened her eyes and gasped as spiders toppled over her head and into the pool, cascading down from the chutes. Their hairy brown legs wiggled as they tried to grasp onto her. She flailed, but one latched onto her left hand and bit through the flesh. Rue screamed and plunged below the water.

When her head resurfaced, all she saw was the calm, ruby drizzle of the fountains. The pool radiated with a dim red hue, and the waves cast moving shadows against the palm fronds.

Her heartbeat thumped in her ears as she felt something slip from between her bare legs into the water below her. A wet and glistening membrane bobbed for a moment, then floated up to the surface. She swam around it, observing the translucent, fleshy exterior and the tiny veins running just below the viscous layer. It looked like hair. Red hair, as wavy as hers once was, inside the round, silken globe.

She drifted closer until she could almost touch its smooth, opaque surface, then pressed a fingertip against it. When it didn't burst, she cupped it in both of her hands. She peered into the haze, trying to make out what hid inside. Then she saw it. The fuzzy-edged shape of a small creature with a delicate face. Two closed eyes and a little bow mouth. It was too murky to see the rest, but she knew that was a child.

Her child? Even if it wasn't, even if she was dreaming, she embraced the fever dream. She hugged the silken globe against her bare chest until she was afraid it would burst.

"Let's go home," she whispered to the globe. "I'll keep you safe. Ron doesn't have to know. No one has to know."

Rue guided the sphere toward the pool steps and held it steady as she crossed the pool deck. Then she placed it delicately on a lounge chair so she could slip on her crochet cover-up. She cradled the sphere in her arms on the walk back home, with elbows dripping. The chlorine smell faded from her hair, but the sphere still clung to the aroma. She pressed her nose against it with each inhale.

* * *

In the morning, Rue woke to a snoring Ron and a drenched

bedspread. Her head felt light and groggy as she peeled herself away from the soaked sheets.

She donned a fresh dress and made her way to the kitchen for a glass of ice water. As she pulled the eggs from the fridge to prepare breakfast, fragments of the strange dream returned. A lump grew in her throat at the memory of a child trapped inside an egg.

Rue guzzled the entire glass. Had it been a dream? She didn't know, but the feeling it left was real. A mix of elation and sadness. Rue glanced down at the spiderweb of veins on her left hand. In the center, two small fang marks punctured the skin.

She rushed to the bathroom, where a large wicker laundry basket sat beside the shower and ripped off the lid. Yes, there was a globe nesting there with the dirty beach towels. Yes, there were two small eyes glancing up at her through the milky viscera. No, it had not been a dream.

Rue fell to her knees beside the laundry basket. "Thank you, thank you, thank you," she whispered.

Of course she had hid the globe in the beach towel bin. Ron would never think to look there. The only time he cared about beach towels was when they were out of clean ones, which was rare. Her baby could be warm and safe in here without fear of being discovered.

Ron called to her from the bedroom in an upset and frantic way. He probably realized the bed sheets were wet again. She would take care of that later.

Rue peered over the side of the basket until the two eyes, blue like hers, swam up again.

"Rue—!" he called again.

"Coming!" She gazed lovingly into the eyes. "I'll be back," she cooed at the baby. "I promise."

When she headed down the hallway and rounded the corner, Ron wasn't staring at the bed sheets. He gazed upward toward the ceiling. Rue cleared her throat in the doorway, and he jumped.

"Get the broom," he instructed, "and something we can sweep it into, like a shoebox."

"Sweep what into a shoebox?"

He pointed at the wall where a crooked brown star of eight legs, at least a couple of inches in diameter, loomed. One of the longer legs helped the spider pivot and dart closer to the ceiling. But it stopped again, realizing it had nowhere to go.

"It's a wolf spider," explained Ron. "We've got to be careful. It could be pregnant. If I swat a pregnant wolf spider, then that's hundreds of baby wolf spiders running through the condo."

Rue chewed at the inside of her cheek but didn't move from the doorway. "You don't say."

"This kind carries them on her back!" he insisted.

"When did you find that out, honey?"

Ron's shoulders slumped and his voice raised at her in irritation. "When I smashed one at the clubhouse right after we moved here. Okay?"

Rue smirked. "You never told me about that."

"Well, you never asked. Now would you get a God damn shoebox or something? Before it runs away!"

She took her time finding an empty shoebox and delivered it to Ron, still frozen in the same spot in the middle of the bedroom. Once she left, the pounding against the wall and curses started. Rue was on her fifth ice cube in the kitchen when Ron reappeared. His brow sweat and wet rings radiated from his armpits. He had his golf bag in his hands, but no shoebox.

"I'm gonna be at the golf course a while," he mumbled. The

door slammed shut behind him.

She knew then that Ron wouldn't be back for hours and that the spider had won. She only hoped the soggy sheets were the only mess left for her to clean up.

After cleaning, she returned to the bathroom and peeled back the woven wicker lid to find the wolf spider sitting on top of the globe. At first she wanted to swat it away, but she realized it was fixated on the globe, as curious about the creature inside as she had been.

The face of the tiny baby cropped up again. First one and then another and then a third. Rue gasped with delight as each of them blinked their sleepy eyes. They must have surfaced to watch the spider, too, as their blurred mouths drew open in awe. Atop their heads were tiny tendrils of hair as fiery and cinnamon as Rue's hair had been once. The hair seemed to float around their misty faces.

One of the spider's thick, hairy front legs flexed back and forth as if to wave hello. Rue was reminded of the black swan pose of the spider in the pool the previous night. Then the faces sank deeper into the globe and disappeared. The spider crawled onto the edge of the wicker basket and turned toward Rue.

Three. Triplets. She couldn't believe it. A smile spread across her face. She lowered a hand toward the wolf spider and let it climb onto her palm. Its furry brown legs tickled. With it so close, she could now see the baby spiders huddled on the wolf spider's back.

"It will be our secret," she told the spider. She carried the mother and babies back to the bedroom. Although she knew it wouldn't stay, she placed it on top of Ron's pillow.

Afternoon showers came and went, but this didn't keep Ron from the golf course. He returned at dusk without a word then shuffled down the hallway and slipped into his pajama pants, as if he knew fresh sheets awaited him. Rue resented this and wished the spider were still on his pillow, crawling over his ear and across his lips. But she knew it wasn't, because he would have screamed.

One day turned into one week, with Rue's secret still safe in the hamper. She kept their pool towels in the linen closet religiously stacked, with just enough left in the hamper to cushion and protect the sphere. But with the pool closed for repairs, it made no sense for Ron to disturb her hiding spot. His visits to the golf course increased instead, as did her time alone at home with the satiny white orb in her lap.

Each night she dreamed she visited the pool again, her bare feet tiptoeing along the pavers and past the yellow tape. Each time a spider would reappear on the perimeter. But instead of an empty pool, bare down to its blue swim lane stripes, red lava water gushed from the fountain brighter than before. Rue didn't think twice before diving in.

And each time she woke in another pool of sweat that fuzzy line between sleep and awake grew fuzzier.

Then one morning Rue woke to the hot sun beating against her skin. Her shoulder blades ached as if she'd slept on concrete all night. She shielded her eyes and squinted, only to be blinded by white light all around her.

When she glanced down, a navy blue line ran between her legs. A wolf spider suddenly materialized from the line. It ran along, then hovered at a distance in front of her. She stood up and walked toward the spider until her eyes adjusted.

Her face lifted to catch the morning light pouring through the treetops. The pool. She had crawled inside of the empty pool sometime during the night. The wolf spider scurried up the deep white wall, onto the tiled edge, then up under the belly of the lifeless fountain.

Rue glanced over her shoulder. The shallow end of the pool felt a mile away. She walked toward the high wall where the spider climbed and placed a hand against it. A gummy feeling slipped from between her fingers and glued her hand to the concrete. She wondered if she was still dreaming, but the squawk of the seagulls above sounded too real. Her other hand pressed into the firm and temperate pool façade. Again, it stuck. She remembered how the spider danced so gracefully across the bedroom wall, even as it ran for its life.

She pushed her body upward until both hands and feet adhered, then crawled higher along the side of the pool. Once she reached the ledge, the gumminess of her palms receded. She never felt lighter and freer than in this moment.

But the joy was shattered by screams, rising faintly in the distance at first. Then they grew heavier, closer, smothering her ears like hot air.

Rue ran to her phone and house keys, resting on one of the few lounge chairs nearby. On the phone's screen was a message from Ron from over an hour ago: *Can this white thing in the hamper be washed with my golf shirts?*

Rue imagined a collapsed orb, the infants with their red hair tangling, and soapy water filling their lungs. Her heart pulsed in her throat. The wolf spider snaked onto the top of her left hand, overlapping each of its legs with the purple veins that twisted beneath her skin.

From around the corner and over the fence they crept on delicate spider legs toward Rue. Bobbing faces with reddish hair, blue eyes, and open-mouthed smiles. She could see them with such clarity now, freed from the misty soup of their globe.

Hundreds of chubby baby faces riding on a sea of spider legs. As she bent down to embraced them, their thick, brown limbs clambered up her arms and torso.

"Oh my girls, my baby girls," she cried out wistfully. "Come to Mama."

Black Moose

In the rearview mirror, Eric watched it follow, with finger-like shadows stretched across the snow. It had been following him since Calcutta, he thought, since he'd turned West and into that snowstorm. Perhaps it was just the telephone lines at an angle on the road behind him. Perhaps he'd been going in circles so long he was seeing things that weren't there. Still, the voices in his head whispered *Run*.

A glaring check engine light on the dash was the only animated thing he'd seen for miles. Yellow ticks along a gray highway drummed past, along with faded green signs for Bear Run or Turkey Creek or Salamander Crossing. But the rest of the landscape was so blinding white, he thought he might go blind.

At night it was so dark the narrow space illuminated by his headlights was all that existed. Last night he'd waited for that moment when another car's headlights would appear in front of him, but that moment never came.

How many miles had he driven? How many days? What was this thing he felt following him? If he had to tell time by the stubble on his face, it would be a week since Calcutta. But then he couldn't remember if he'd shaved the day he fled. He knew he'd stopped once or twice to wipe piled-up snow off the passenger seat and to stare at the picture of his wife and son pinched into the cupholder. But he couldn't remember much of the rest. Stopping to let the worst of the storm pass. Stopping to pee. Taking bites from a candy bar he found in the center console until only one piece remained. Now that piece was frozen stiff against the bottom of the cup holder.

His dashboard had gone almost completely silent after the snowstorm died down. First, he lost the GPS, then the radio, then the digital clock, and now the gas gauge hovered just above empty. The horizon had already suffocated the sun and bled out twilight. He dreaded another night.

Then the faded image of a red wrench materialized at the side of the road. Eric passed it at first, believing he was hallucinating this, too, after making a creature from the shadows along the highway. But just a few yards farther, he slowed the car down and turned around. He didn't trust he'd find another sign of life anytime soon.

The wheels of his car bumped against the curb in front of the repair garage. Below the red wrench, the sign said Wreck 'n Stuff. He wondered at the name. What was the 'stuff' part? Or was it a play on words—wrecking stuff?

Wind poured into the lap of the empty passenger seat through a large hole in the windshield above it. It was shaped like a snowflake, with dark red along the tips of the broken glass. He would say a deer darted in front of him if one of the shop guys asked. Out in these parts, they'd believe him.

Eric released the steering wheel from his grip and plucked the photograph of his wife and son from the center console. Her dark hair was in ribbon curls, with a center streak of white combed to one side. His son, so young, also had a shock of white cutting through his hair. They were both smiling, and he was pretty sure it was because he wasn't in the photo. She blamed him before she left, saying the stress caused the white, like bombing victims in the Second World War or Marie Antoinette in the flight to Varennes. That's what she compared him to. World Wars. Beheadings.

A cold fog escaped his nostrils, and he thrust the photo into his coat pocket. Under florescent lights sat a single gas pump. A sign that read 'See clerk' was taped to the screen. He turned again toward the garage, where dim lights peeked through window blinds. The sign in the front window said it was open, but he wondered if that were true. If they'd closed, he would sleep in the car until the next morning, even if it meant frostbite. He had no other choice.

Eric combed the insides of his coat pockets but couldn't feel his pistol. He glanced in the back seat, where his duffle bag should have been. No gun there either. Just an empty, stained polyester cover. His left eye began to twitch, as it often did when he felt stressed. He cursed himself for not keeping the gun close by.

He stepped out of the vehicle into the frigid wind and pulled his coat into his chest. The only sound he heard was his own breathing and the gentle patter of snowflakes against the roof of the car. No more screams. No more "Please, Daddy. I promise I won't tell."

Maybe it was better this way.

When he pressed the fob, he heard the trunk release, but it didn't pop open. He cursed again, and when no amount of tugging broke it free of the ice, he slammed a fist against it.

Then he heard a few soft crunches behind him, like footsteps in the snow. Long, shadowy fingers stretched beside the car and stopped. It was behind him. He knew it. He could hear it breathe. He scrambled toward the shop door, thankful the handle turned in his grip.

Bells jingled just above his head inside the door. There was a long counter illuminated by a single, dangling bulb across from him. Behind it, the faces and torsos of two bears emerged. Neither moved. Eric blinked back the shadows as more animal silhouettes appeared along the wall. A coyote with a rabbit dangling from its mouth. Fish in graduated sizes, like an aquarium along the wall. Deer. Armadillos. This must be the stuff of Wreck 'n Stuff, he thought. Stuffed, as in taxidermy.

In the center of it all stood a woman as rigid as the rest. Eric's throat clenched when their eyes met. Something about her was unappealing. She wore gray plaid and a black apron. Her skin was pale, almost as pale as the snow outside, and her hair was auburn, pulled into a ponytail. He couldn't tell if she was young or old. But her nose was high in the air, as if she'd smelled him coming.

She didn't budge as Eric closed the door behind him. He kept a grip on the handle, wondering if she, too, were stuffed. "You open?" he called out. "My windshield is broken. I just—I can't keep driving with it like that, and I'm out of gas."

The woman blinked twice but said nothing. She crept slowly from around the counter until they were shoulder to shoulder, then she pressed the tip of her nose against the window and stared outside. Now that she was closer, he could tell she was middle aged, like him. She smelled of soot and plastic. The whole place did.

"That yours?" she asked, pointing at his vehicle. Her voice had some twang in it.

Eric frowned. "Of course. Aren't I the only one here?"

She clicked her tongue disapprovingly and trotted back toward the counter. "We close in 20. But if you hang around for 30, I can drive you to a motel a mile south of here and bring you back tomorrow for the fix."

"Wait. You're the one who fixes the cars?" he asked skeptically.

She harrumphed. "Well, ain't I the only one here?"

Eric swallowed his frustration. Better to lay low and play dumb than piss off the only person who could get him out of this mess. He peered over his shoulder and out the window. The long shadows were still there, stretched like veins or tree limbs across the parking lot from seemingly nowhere.

He cleared his throat and turned back to the clerk. "I mean, isn't there a way you could fix it tonight? I'm kind of in a hurry."

"Look," she sighed, "it ain't happening tonight. That windshield's gonna take at least an hour, and we close in 20. Everything around here's closed except the motel." She popped open the register and started counting change. "And you're dumber than you look if you think you're gonna walk from here to there in the snow," she mumbled.

Eric tried to keep calm, but warm blood crawled up the back of his neck. "I didn't see any hotel on that road. Just this place."

Her eyes lifted. "That a question or an accusation? If you don't want my help, man, then take your broken windshield and go somewhere else."

Eric thought of the shadows beside the car, what might be waiting for him if he went back out there alone. His left eyelid jerked. "I'm sorry," he said. "It's been a long day. I got caught in that snowstorm and got all turned around. You're right. I need a hotel room and my car fixed. I just hoped I could do those in reverse order. I didn't mean to offend you."

This made her smile. "Now that's more like it, mister."

She pointed to a tiny badge embroidered on her black apron. "Name's Kris, with a 'K.' What's yours?"

He thought to lie, but then he thought of the moment he would need to show his driver's license or sign for the repairs. *Haste makes waste*, his wife always said. He was a fucking idiot for not keeping more cash on hand. "Name's Eric."

"Eric, where you from? I can't place your accent."

This time he lied. "Trenton." It sounded common enough.

She kept her head down, shuffling the fat quarters into her palm. "Never heard of it. Must've come a long way."

He nodded.

She gestured at the door. "Could you flip that sign for me? So no one else thinks I can work 20-minute miracles?"

He walked back over to the entrance and flipped the sign, trying to stay out of view of the window frame. But when he paused, he swore he heard crunching just outside the door. When he turned back around, Kris was gone.

A clang sounded from a backroom. "Don't mind me!" he heard her yell. "Hey, you want something to eat or drink?"

"Coffee would be great," he yelled back. "Black. And if you have any food back there, I'd appreciate it."

"Won't coffee keep you up?" she yelled.

"At this rate, nothing will."

Eric paced along the walls and back to the counter. He peered up at the two frozen bears. One disappeared at the waist into the wooden wall panels. It bared its teeth, and its paws stretched outward, as if it were about to grab him. The other was more docile. Ears perked high and a look of curiosity in its dark glass eyes. Its paws rested on the fake tree branch attached just below its torso.

Eric was reminded of the small brown bear his son nuzzled

into tatters. Brownie, he called it, because it was brown. Was that in the duffle bag in the trunk, too?

Kris reappeared from a backroom in a red hunting vest that added bulk to her midsection. She handed him a steaming cup of black coffee and a pack of peanut butter crackers.

"Thanks. I was wondering," Eric said as he sipped the coffee, "how does one end up fixing cars and also . . . this?" He gestured toward the bears.

"Taxidermy? You'd be surprised. Same materials. Bondo, for example. It's a plastic filler for cars but makes for good ear work on whitetail, too." She shrugged. "It's an economical pairing. What can I say?"

She pulled out a rag to dust off a large alabaster-colored head under the faded bulb. It was shaped like a camel but with a waddle under its neck. Its eyes were formless and blank. White knobs on a white skull.

"What's that?" he asked.

"A moose head. Hard to recognize without the antlers, right? It's just a mount for the skin. There's a lot of moose around here, but they're hard to catch. I've been holding onto this mount for years." She tucked the rag into her pocket and stared lovingly at the skinless mannequin. "One day I'm gonna get him."

"Him?" asked Eric. "There's only one moose?"

She rolled her eyes. "Of course not, but there's only one moose I care about." She lowered her voice and glanced around the room, as if she didn't want the other animals to hear. "This fella, he's big. Ten feet tall at the shoulders. Thirteen with the head and horns. But the weird thing, the weird thing about him, Eric, is no one's ever seen him alive—unless they're going to die.

"First, they see only his shadow. Antlers creeping up wherever they go. Feels like something's following them."

Eric realized he was sweating. A cold, damp sweat. He wiped his brow. If she was playing with him, if this was some kind of prank, he'd wrap his hands around her throat.

She continued, "I thought it was folklore until my husband saw it. For a few agitated days and sleepless nights, he kept talking about the shadow that followed him. Then he told me, 'The Black Moose is coming to get me, Kris.' And then it got him. The next morning, he swerved off a cliff and into the arms of Turkey Creek."

"Jesus." Eric's left eye began to quiver. "What caused him to swerve?"

Her serious face cracked with a smile. "I'm just messing with you. My husband's dead, yes, but he careened into a tree to avoid a moose in the road. Seventy miles an hour." She shelved the dustless mannequin head and stared at him. "That what happened to you?"

His heart pulsed in his ears. "Happened to me?"

"Your windshield. You hit a moose? You seem shook up all of a sudden." She took off her apron and set it on the counter. "I really did scare you with the story, didn't I? The kids made it up around a campfire one year. Scared the shit out of me the first time I heard it, too."

Eric imagined the concentric circles of broken glass radiating from one dense point above the passenger seat, just wide enough for a forehead, and the blood that darkened from a sticky crimson red to a snow-tipped maroon.

"I can't remember much about what happened, honestly," he lied.

"Well, you're lucky you walked away alive," she said.

"Could've been worse. You swerved just in time or that moose would've been in your lap. Could've been a deer, though. Less damage. Hard to tell after the fact, unless you see the body, though." She eyed him. "Did you see the body?"

Eric's left eyelid trembled uncontrollably.

Kris watched as he tugged at the lashes. "Sorry, man. I can tell talking about it upsets you. Let's just get you to that hotel, where you can catch a good night's rest. Tomorrow I'll get to work on your car." She extended an open hand. "Done with your coffee?"

"A few more sips to go," he said.

"Then let's top it off and lid it on the way out."

Kris led him to the back door, and they climbed into the cabin of a tow truck parked behind the garage. He scanned the lot as they drove off, searching for the antlers, as the last drop of hot coffee hit his belly. Kris had turned on the heat, but Eric still felt a chill he couldn't shake each time he glanced in the rearview mirror.

Along the highway, the snowflakes grew thick as they rushed past the truck's narrow head beams. They made no small talk, but Kris peered over at him several times on the drive. "Anyone ever tell you that you look familiar?" she asked. "Like that celebrity. What's his name?"

Eric shifted beneath her gaze. All he wanted to do was sleep. "I don't watch much TV. Can't help you there." He yawned and felt the tension of the day escaping from his muscles.

Kris clicked her tongue. "Right. I'll place it sooner or later."

They drove the rest of the way in silence.

* * *

Eric woke with a piercing headache and thought he must've fallen asleep on the way to the motel. He didn't remember checking in, didn't remember the bed, bathroom, or alarm clock. He hoped he hadn't missed his ride back to the garage this morning. It hurt to think.

An eerie silence rang in his ears, and when he opened his eyes, he was met with blinding light. It took several blinks until he could make out a landscape of snow before him. He couldn't lift his head. His skull felt like it would crack each time he moved his neck.

Something pressed against his cheek then, and he shifted his gaze. A giant black moose stared down at him with wet, dark eyes. The flap of skin just below its neck swayed. Above the moose's head were bloody horns that reached into the sky. Skin dangled off them, like red velvet, a webwork of veins nested in the flesh.

Kris's voice surfaced somewhere in the distance. It was faint at first, then clearer as she approached him. "Too bad about that snowstorm, huh? The authorities thought you'd have crossed the border into Canada by now. But lucky for everyone, you got little sidetracked here."

Eric titled his head in the direction of Kris's voice and found a gun resting in her hands. His gun, from the trunk of the car. His heart quickened. Cold breath spilled from his nostrils and mouth.

"I had a hunch the minute I saw your car. Same make and model that's been all over the news," she said. "The police are on their way right now, of course. But we know we can't rely on the law to serve justice these days." She pulled some shells from the pocket of her red vest and checked the barrel. "By the way, nice pistol, Eric."

Eric scrambled under the weight of his skull, as if his head was tied to bricks. His hands reached upward and grasped onto two long, bony protrusions that stuck out from his temples. He ran his fingers along their length until their forms split once and again. At the base of each, thick wire wove into his scalp, securing the mounts. When he drew back his hands, they were covered in blood and hair.

"Don't ruin them," Kris warned. "I spent most of the morning sewing and gluing those to your thick skull. I knew I'd make use of those extra antlers someday. Now get up."

Tears welled in his eyes. "But—"

"Grab the antlers by their base to steady them and get your ass on up here, Eric."

He grasped each antler and lifted until he was sitting upright. Then he maneuvered his legs underneath him so he could stand. The cold made him shake, and every movement threatened to topple him over again.

Kris chuckled as she watched.

The black moose sniffed him from his pant legs to his crown. Its ears perked up.

"B-but wait," he stuttered. "D-don't you see it? R-right there."

"See what?" She scanned the landscape around them and returned her eyes to him. "Don't try anything tricky."

"The moose! The black moose! He's standing right here." He tried to gesture with one of his hands, but quickly gripped the mount at his skull again.

"You really are loony tunes, mister," Kris said. "I told you last night that was a story, nothing but folklore. And now you're trying to game me with it. That moose is about as real as your chances of seeing the sunset again." He heard a click.

"No, please. I swear." His lower lip quivered. The black moose blew hot air against his cheek.

"So you're saying I'm supposed to believe a guy who ploughs his car into his ex-wife while his kid watches, then stuffs the kid into his car trunk and leaves him there to die." She spit into the snow between them. "He was still alive when I found him, you know? Barely. Starving, dehydrated, unable to speak because he screamed himself hoarse. But alive. There's frostbite, though. Probably have to have something amputated. His whole future is fucked because of you."

Eric felt blood and sweat trickle down his forehead.

"So this is what we're going to do," she said. "I'll give you a head start. Now I'm an expert marksman, and with those antlers I sewed into your skull, you ain't going to get very far very fast. But we're gonna have fun trying, okay? On the count of three."

"No, wait. I can explain. This whole thing. You wouldn't believe what she accused me of."

The moose turned away from him and toward the sunrise.

"Whatever it was, she was probably right. Now get going." She pointed the gun at his chest. "One."

Eric turned around slowly and wobbled forward, stumbled, and got back up. He felt like his scalp was going to rip off clean. Droplets of blood fell from his crown, staining the snow at his footsteps an icy maroon, just like the windshield, just like his wife's forehead when it slammed into the glass.

"Two."

The black moose galloped ahead into the vast snowy land-scape, heels kicking behind it in long, graceful strides until it disappeared.

"But it was real," Eric whispered. "I saw it."

A shot rang through the quiet morning.

119

Why She Dreams of Alligators

Amie woke in a puddle of her own sweat, chin propped on her pillow, fingers splayed beside her hips. The doctor had ruled out early menopause despite her nocturnal hot flashes. Instead, his diagnosis blamed the divorce proceedings and custody battle for her angst, along with a suggestion that she see a therapist. Each night Amie experienced predatory dreams of alligators, their glassy eyes blinking at her just before their jaws opened. Each night she resurfaced with every part of her body, from scalp to pelvis, drenched and the bed sheets soaked through to the mattress.

Amie pulled herself up on her knees and wrung droplets from her brown hair, then pried herself from the wet, clinging sheets. She striped the bed, cracking her jaw and neck on both sides to alleviate the pain of her contorted sleep.

Above the laundry room, Amie heard the patter of feet in their groggy march from bedroom to bathroom. Minas, her son. Pancakes were his favorite breakfast, but they were short on time this morning. She browned toast, trimming off the crust and carving a heart through the center, then decorated both the hollowed-out toast and heart with peanut butter and banana slices. Beside the plate, a glass of milk.

Min appeared, wiping sleep from his eyes with one hand and

passing a piece of paper to his mother with the other. He bit into the toast with soft crunching sounds as she examined the paper. Another monster. This time the head of a crocodile with a full lion's mane and a stubby-tailed, claw-footed rear end. At least that's what the crayon scratches appeared to be.

This routine of the past insufferable months included twice weekly ventures to her lawyer and her therapist—sometimes consecutive—all while balancing four days together with her toddler son and three days without him. The days without were hardest.

Min, too, required a therapist to weather an unsettling muteness that had befallen him. Because his father, Nick, refused to subtract an hour of therapy from any of his days with Min, Amie interrupted at least one of her own to take him.

In the words of her therapist: It's no wonder she had night-mares.

The boy paused to look up from his toast and clapped his hands together, pulling Amie from her trance. Amie smiled, kissed his forehead, and whispered "Good work, Min" into his ear. She grabbed a magnet from the refrigerator door and hung this monster beside the others—an ogre with its red tongue protruding, horned creatures with no faces, birds with eyes drawn so dark it felt as if those eyes followed her. But the therapist assured her these monsters embodied Min's unspoken feelings, his anger over the separation. She should invite them, celebrate them even, despite their fearful appearances.

In the words of her son's therapist: It's not like he's drawn a murder.

Amie understood Min was angry. She was angry, too.

The list of abuses grew too long to ignore: Nick telling Min he had to 'earn' his bath time and sending him to bed dirty and crying. Nick impersonating and tormenting Min over his stutter, sometimes refusing to acknowledge the boy when it happened, until Min shook before he spoke to anyone. So Amie fled with Min one morning as Nick stood in the middle of the road, his middle finger pointed at the car, his silver wedding band glinting beside it. Nick reported Amie's license plate, accused her of child abduction. When they caught her and Min at the Florida-Georgia line, she countered with child abuse. But had no evidence to prove either, so no immediate decision resulted. Their characters were both in question, though. The lines drawn in the sand. Nick's lawyer served her with divorce papers while they were separated, just days before her own lawyer would have hers ready.

Amie stepped outside to light a cigarette while Min finished dressing and slipped on his shoes. She took a drag. The weather vane mounted on the roof pointed East today, in a cloudless blue sky. Its copper scales-of-justice design with a gavel in place of an arrow didn't fit with their gated community's ambience, immaculate yards, or conservative veneers. She'd half wondered if she'd receive a letter in the mail asking her to remove it. But the weather vane was a gift from her neighbor, a member of the homeowners' association, who had also been through a divorce. The neighbor once overheard Nick on the driveway cursing at Amie. Another time she saw him strike Min on the back of the head. So the minute the separation gossip reached the neighbors ears, she brought the weather vane over.

"May he be reminded of the judicial hell you're about to put him through every time his car pulls up to the house," she said.

Today, Amie and Min would take a wildlife airboat ride through the marshlands of Florida to see the alligators. Amie hated alligators. But Min loved them. He'd fallen into the age of toddler obsessions, and alligators topped the list. He even had a plastic alligator toy with paddling feet that joined him everywhere.

She'd read once that alligators were more closely related to birds than lizards. But, to her, they were absent of the grace and vulnerability that made birds attractive.

Min appeared from behind the front door with toy alligator in hand. She walked him to the car.

An hour and two breakfast cookies later, they arrived at the airboats. The website promised an experience of a lifetime, matched by pictures to prove it. Little boys holding tape-mouthed alligators in both their hands. Smiles on faces and hair whipped back as the airboats cut through shallow river waters. But Amie wondered, given the minimal parking and car shelter beside the souvenir shop, if they could deliver on their promise.

She paid at the register inside of the shop and fiddled with the cigarette pack in her pants pocket. Min sat on the floor beside a giant potbelly pig with a collar that read Hamlet. The wheezing whispers of sleep coming from the pig's nose and mouth entranced him. Amie asked if it was okay to step out for a moment while her son played with the pig. The woman at the register nodded, as if she was asked this question daily.

"Be good, Min," Amie instructed. "I'll be right back."

She stayed close, still able to see glimmers of Min and the sleeping pig between shelves while she paced along the front deck. She could feel her heartbeat quicken at the thought of seeing a gator up close. Maybe too close. Before she knew it, she'd smoked the cigarette down to the butt.

The powerful, whirring start of the airboat fans at the docks in the back sounded. Amie extinguished the butt with her sneaker and walked around toward the docks.

Min stood at the front of the line already, getting an orange life jacket cinched around his torso by an employee. The headphones were larger than his head. Apart from them, an elderly woman and what appeared to be her son, as well as two young women snapping selfies with their phones, stood in line. Min grabbed Amie's hand and pulled her into the wide stadium seating of the boat. She let him sit at the edge, one hand gripping the silver bars and head poking through it.

Their airboat pilot was young, with sandy blond hair peeking out from beneath his camouflage ballcap. "Check. Check. Can everyone hear me?"

The adults raised their thumbs in the air. Min readjusted his oversize headphones and turned to Amie with a smile.

"Here's the deal. I'll do the spotting. You all handle the oohs and ahhs when we get there," said the pilot. "Roger?"

"Roger!" everyone yelled into their mics.

And it was true. Whenever the pilot spotted a gator—a muddy green body along the muddy green banks of the river—he'd announce it. The rest of them could never see what he was talking about when he pointed. Then the airboat would hover at rapid speed toward some isolated spot along the marsh. With noise cut and boat still, the riders tilted toward each gator and snapped photos. They gripped each other's arms and whispered things like "That's a big one." The gators, if they moved at all, kept their distance from the boat and slunk among the cattle that grazed in the marshes. Still, Amie kept her eye on Min instead of the alligators, ready to match his expression each time he turned around. No words of joy passed his lips, but she'd learned to interpret his silence.

Just before the end of their time, the young pilot let them drift toward a swampier section of the river, where Cypress trees stretched toward the sky, their long, knobby knees just above brown water. It was darker here, eerie at the water's edge. Spanish moss entangled through the branches, creating a canopy that blocked the sun. Amie listened for the sound of birds but didn't hear any.

"There's one," the pilot said, pointing toward Min's side of the boat. "We'll just steer toward it a bit."

The boat inched closer and stalled. Amie and Min both leaned in. A brown nose surfaced, like damaged leather on the toe of a men's wide work boot. Behind it, two dark orbs blinked and stared at Amie. She held her breath. The gator leapt from the water and lunged at the side of the airboat, never breaking contact with Amie's eyes. Amie pulled on Min, and he jumped into her lap.

Through the headphones, they heard laughter. "Aw, she's just fussing, folks. Nothing to be worried about. They can't get us up here," the pilot assured them. "But it's just past mating season, so she's probably got eggs back behind there. Protective mama. Let's give her some space."

Amie heard the throb of her heart in her ears. As she clutched Min, she felt his heart flutter, too. But when he turned his head, his expression was elated. If he could speak, he would have said "Again!" She couldn't mirror his feelings, though. Her whole body began to sweat.

Min slipped back into his seat, and Amie clutched the cigarette carton in her pocket all the way back to the docks.

* * *

When Nick came to pick up Min, he passed Amie a letter informing her of his request for full custody of their son. Amie knew Nick had the upper financial hand in this battle—bigger paycheck, bigger house, bigger lawyer. After she read through the letter on the living room couch, she ripped it apart, pretending it was Nick's neck. She wanted to tear him to pieces the way he had torn apart their lives.

When she called her attorney, his recommendations read like an overhaul of her life: find a full-time job, make a record of all the times in the past six months when she'd taken Min to the doctor or child psychologist or cared for him when he was sick, gather photos of all the times she'd taken him on trips, like the one to the airboat ride—a photo Amie failed to capture. Then gather bank records for all the money she'd spent on these trips, record a testimonial from the neighbor who gave her the weather vane, buy a calendar and document everything she did from here forward in the name of Min.

Angrily, Amie wondered why she couldn't also provide to the court the nine months of pregnancy and fourteen hours of labor she'd devoted in the name of Min. Her attorney laughed then reiterated his point. She wanted to strangle him also. Instead, she spent every extra hour of her days recording what she could remember and planning the next outing she'd share with Min.

The night before Nick was supposed to bring Min back, a new nightmare surfaced. It opened at the lake just behind the neighborhood homes. Amie remembered being in the lake water, neck deep, peering toward the back of their house. The sun had already set, painting a soft red tinge over every surface. Brick pavers stretched from the dock up a small hill toward the home's pool. Inside its screened enclosure, something splashed. Amie assumed it was Min in the dream, although she couldn't see or hear him from the lake. Her heart raced. When her eyes traveled back to her side, Amie's hair stood on end.

Floating around her were dozens of red eyes. Two by two, just drifting slowly along the water's dark surface. More alligators. She wanted to scream, but when she opened her mouth, no sound escaped. Then something butted against the middle of Amie's back. She whirled around, and an enormous gator, with a cigarette trapped between its teeth, stared her in the face.

Then the dream ended.

Amie woke on the dock behind the house. This bothered her because she'd never sleepwalked before. She reached a hand to her scalp and felt dampness. Her nightgown was soaked through, as if she'd just emerged from the water. Amie swore she also saw dozens of bubbles appear and pop beside the dock. Final breaths of the alligators before they submerged? Amie shuddered at the thought.

She clung to her therapist's advice as she rushed up the brick path toward the house: Dreams are the gray area between the conscious and subconscious. What you experience isn't real, no matter how real it feels.

All she wanted was to get into fresh clothes before Nick dropped off Min. But Nick was already wrapping at the front door when she entered the house. Amie's hand gripped the doorknob. When she swung the door open, Nick's face fell flat.

"Jesus, Amie. Take a dip in the pool this morning?"

She forced a smile. "Long story. Come here, Min." She coaxed him inside and slammed the door shut on Nick.

Min crouched on the foyer floor and immediately unpacked his bag.

"Not here, babe. Can we take that to your bedroom?"

Min unpacked faster. He dug for something buried inside. Then a slip of paper escaped from between his hands onto the floor. Amie cocked her head at a sketch of what appeared to be a bathtub, jagged water drawn inside, and a boy like Min bobbing in the water. Beside him swam a baby alligator. Min lifted the drawing from the floor and handed it to Amie.

She smiled because, unlike Min's other drawings, there was a normalcy to this one. Cute even. The trip on the airboat must have inspired him.

"How sweet. Thank you, Min." She ran her fingers through his hair, and they walked together to the refrigerator, where Amie placed another magnet on the drawing. "Mommy needs to change so we can go on another adventure. Will you clean up your backpack while I get ready?"

Min's eyes widened at the word 'adventure,' and he nodded yes.

* * *

At the entrance to Gator World, visitors were required to pass through the open jaws and gutted body of a fake, two-story alligator. Amie held her breath as they passed teeth half her height. Min ran ahead.

A raised board navigated around the entire park. In pools beside them, dozens of gators snaked around each other under the shade of a rustic cabana, while others lounged across a wooden deck in shallow water. They lay in piles in the heat, their fat baby arms crawling over turtle shells and each other's backs. Slender white egrets tiptoed around them. Occasionally one would lift its head and open its jaws into a yawn.

Amie bent down to get her phone out of her purse to snap a few shots with Min, then noticed through the gaps of the boards a smaller gator hovering in the water just below them. A pink, fleshy slash was drawn across the gator's nose. Uneasy, Amie guided Min to another part of the boardwalk, where no gators seemed to be swimming. Min gave his best cheese, and when Amie checked the photo, she saw the gator with the pink scar behind them. She turned. Indeed, the alligator lingered at the corner of this pond and watched.

They continued along the winding decks toward an aviary and snake exhibition. Amie couldn't shake the feeling of the pink-nosed gator's eyes upon her, of all their eyes. As she moved, the gators sensed her approaching, turned to meet her, and followed her footsteps. The image of the gator leaping toward the airboat flashed through her mind, and she squeezed Min's hand.

"How you doing, Min? Is this fun?"

Min looked up at her then back at his feet.

"What's wrong, babe?"

Then they heard the clang of a bell, and a man with a thick Southern drawl called out. "Feeding time! Everybody git 'round!"

Min pulled her toward the edge of the deck into a crowd of people. They gathered around two men dressed in overalls and white T-shirts. The men carried big buckets onto a closed-off deck surrounded by hungry alligators. They exchanged jokes while dangling full-size chicken carcasses over the water. The gators raised their snouts in the air, feet climbing along each other's braille backs, until one jumped from the water to catch a chicken leg between its teeth.

A woman behind them offered to take a photo of Amie and Min during the show. Amie lifted Min to her hip as the woman counted to three several times. When they finished, Amie turned to find the pink-nosed gator drifting from the pack and making a beeline for her. She tried to back away as the gator approached but bumped into a man standing behind her. The phone slipped from her hand and clinked against the wooden rail then plopped into the water.

The pink-nosed gator swam closer. Amie watched as its mouth unfastened and swallowed her phone.

* * *

Back at home, she pulled the car into the driveway and spotted Nick running from behind the house.

"Amie! There's a goddamn gator in the pool! Help!"

Amie locked the car doors and stared as Nick went on a crazy tirade. When Nick realized they weren't getting out to help, he slammed his fist on the hood.

"You stay here," she instructed Min. "Don't get out until Mommy or someone you trust says it's okay to come out. I'll leave the engine on." She signaled him to lock the doors behind her.

She managed to remain calm in front Min, but the minute they were out of his sight, she exploded at Nick.

"What the fuck are you doing here when we're not home? That's fucking trespassing!"

"I called, but you didn't pick up," he insisted. Amie imagined the phone vibrating in the pink-nosed alligator's gut. "And it's not trespassing if I paid for the place. It's still mine until the court says it's not."

"Oh, fuck you, Nick."

"Look, are we going to argue about why I'm here or get this fucking gator out of the pool? You're both lucky I was here at all. What if Min just jumped in after you got home?

Amie followed Nick through the screen door and glanced

around the pool deck. The midday sun created a distorted shadow of the screened enclosure. But no gator. Not even traces of splashed water beside the pool. The only movement was the pool vacuum, puttering along the pool floor and walls.

Amie crossed her arms. "Nick!"

"I swear it was here!" he yelled. "At least nine feet, at the deep end of the pool."

"Well, it's not here now. Why were you messing around back here anyway?"

"Min forgot his gator toy," Nick said. "The one with the paddling feet? The one he drags everywhere?"

"I know which toy, Nick. You don't have to talk to me like I'm an idiot. You could have left it by the door with a note. I swear, if you ever come on this property again, I'm gonna—"

Nick raised his hands and laughed. "You're gonna what?"

She swallowed hard. "I'm gonna tell the court you trespassed today because you're seeing things. That you're either a crazy stalker or on drugs—because that's sure what it looks like to me!"

Nick's face changed, and she immediately regretted showing him her cards. He'd have time to devise his own plan, his own excuse, to contradict her.

Nick leaned down into her face, and she was reminded of the alligators from her dream. "Tell them what you want. I have enough money—and the lawyer—to buy me out of anything. By the time I'm done with you, you'll wish you were the one who was crazy." He sneered and brushed past her. On his way out, he brandished his middle finger, that silver wedding band still gleaming beside it. "Enjoy your final days with Min," he called over his shoulder.

Amie's eyes were daggers at his back. She felt hot tears of rage surfacing. As she followed him toward the front of the house, she wiped the tears away. His neck, so delicate and exposed above his shoulders. She wanted to run toward it, to sink her fingernails in the flesh, to rip him to shreds. She watched as Nick tapped on the passenger side of the car and instructed Min to get out to kiss him goodbye. Min shook his head through the window until Nick gave up and drove off.

That night Amie emailed her attorney about the lost phone and searched the web for ways to fight a custody battle. She sat in the kitchen while Min doodled at a small table beside her. When her attorney replied, questioning how she could be so careless and stressing how she was losing time, Amie's head sunk into her hands. She tried not to sob, but she couldn't help it. She was a bad mother. She was going to lose her son.

Min pushed his chair back and rose from his toddler table and walked toward her with another piece of paper. He stood beside her for several moments as she cried. Then he placed a hand on her knee, and she turned to him.

"It's okay, Min. Mommy will be okay. I'm just really, really tired. What do you have there?"

She scooped him into her lap and lifted the paper as she brushed the curls off his forehead. Another gator, with a fat box of a body and four thin lines for legs. Triangles climbed along the gator's back, with a larger triangle at the rear for a tail. The lengthy rectangular jaws opened to expose jagged triangular teeth inside, all colored green. One red eyeball, poised above the body, fixated on her. And in its mouth, the alligator held another long rectangular shape—colored white. The end near the mouth was beige. Crayon circles, like smoke, were drawn at the other end.

The previous night, Min was in her dreams. Somehow, he had

seen it. Beside the alligator was the sketch of a heart with little darts of red spilling out the bottom. The heart was positioned so close to the gator's open mouth, Amie couldn't help but wonder.

It's not like he's drawing a murder, the therapist had said.

Amie covered and uncovered her mouth. "What did you see?" she asked. "Please, Min. Why are the alligators coming for me? What did Mommy do?"

She watched the boy crawl inside himself and divert his eyes. He looked like a robot shutting down. "Min, please. This picture—Mommy loves it. I just need to know what happened. Was Mommy in the lake behind the house the other night? Were there gators? What did you see?"

Min vigorously shook his head until she let him down. Then he ran toward the bathroom. As he shuffled down the hall, he stripped off his clothes, leaving jeans and a Gator World souvenir shirt in his wake. When she heard a faucet flip on, Amie followed him. She found him naked in a stream of bathtub water.

"Okay. Okay," Amie whispered, sinking to her knees beside him. "We can bathe and then get ready for bed. Just let Mommy grab one thing."

She fetched the alligator toy Nick left by the pool, shampooed Min's hair, and soaped up his back. He calmed in the warm bathtub water, winding up the plastic alligator and watching it swim from end to end. They stayed until the water turned lukewarm, until Min could barely keep his eyes open.

Amie cried herself to sleep, wondering how many more of these nights she'd have with her son. In her dreams, the plastic alligator toy came to life as a baby gator, swimming in the bathtub with him. In spite of her fears, she was able to scoop it out of the water, one hand cupping its jaw, the other supporting its warm belly in her palm. The baby gator didn't resist or squirm. It let her carry it all the way to the lake behind the house. As she released it, its slender tail shimmied into the water with a ripple.

When Amie awoke, her skin and scalp were dry against the bed sheets for once. The warm sun poured through her window blinds. She stretched and tiptoed to Min's room to stir him awake. Maybe they'd make pancakes this morning. Maybe they'd go to the park. She sat on the bed and tapped his shoulder until his eyes blinked open.

But his face, that sweet, groggy baby face, curled into terror as he stared. Amie turned toward the full-length mirror beside his bed. And there, caught between her teeth, were two fingers. One long middle finger, dangling from the knuckle. One with a silver wedding band that dropped to the floor. Both dripped blood.

Min opened his mouth and screamed—the first sound he'd made in months.

Lovely

Lizette stared at the reflection of a small nodule on her chin so intently, she missed Dot's calls from the kitchen.

"Yoo-hoo?" Dot came around the bathroom corner clanging her fingertips against an empty wine glass. "What's wrong?"

Lizette let out a sigh and covered her chin with her hand. "Nothing. Well, something. It's always something."

Dot nodded. "Something a big bottle of Moscato can't fix?" She winked.

"No." Lizette smiled. "But I don't want to burden you with it. Offering up your beach cottage so I can . . ." she grasped for the right word, "recover means so much. I don't want to spoil it."

Dot pulled her in for a firm, loving hug and released her. "Divorce is hard. You needed an escape! No one rents the beach house during shoulder season anyway. It's already a bit chilly out there, so I threw some extra blankets on our chairs."

Lizette followed Dot through the modest living room, with its plush, teal loveseat and flamingo paintings, to a large deck. The beach beyond it was hidden by tall, swaying grass, already browning at the tips. But she still smelled the waves, musty yet warm and ripe with salt. When she was younger, trips to the beach always made her want to fall asleep afterward. She pulled the scent through her nostrils until it filled her mouth, and she knew she'd sleep well tonight.

The women walked along the boardwalk to an open beach, where a picnic sat beneath a cream-colored umbrella.

"You shouldn't have!" Lizette gasped.

Dot poured the sparkling, sweet wine and toasted her. "To your newfound freedom!"

Once the sun dipped down, the sky grew overcast and the pale blue waters turned choppy and green. But a sliver of the horizon stayed pink, occasionally dotted with blue bolts of lightning that crept closer.

"I just realized we haven't seen a single person all afternoon," Lizette said.

"That's the appeal. It's not a private beach, per se, but having so few cottages around here makes it feel like one. All the neighbors keep residence in the city and rent out space, just like Forest and me." Dot cleared her throat. "But you can always catch the trolley to downtown for some nightlife. The locals are older, like us. Maybe you'll even meet a new someone while you're here." She shot Lizette a sly smile.

"No, no. I'm done with all that. I'm still processing finding my husband cheating with a woman young enough to be my grandchild. What I need is more Moscato, not another man in a midlife crisis." But even as she said it, Lizette felt a piece of her heart crack. Her voice became soft and disconnected then. "You should see her Instagram. She's a model. Fashionable, perfect body, and here I am with menopause acne on my first vacation in years."

"Nonsense. You're gorgeous! His loss!" Dot insisted. "Besides, they always say you meet someone when you're not looking." She took a long sip.

Lizette reached for her own glass, but the wind kicked up, and she caught a face full of sand instead. She spat and rubbed the tender cyst along her chin, burning with irritation.

"We better get back inside," Dot advised. "These storms can creep up quickly." She stacked the plates and headed toward the tall beach grass, Lizette close behind her with their Moscato.

In the bathroom, as she washed her hands, Lizette heard the tinkling of rain above. She leaned in closer to the mirror until she saw a small, white particle in the center of the zit. Not a pustule or head but a grain of sand, stuck like a seed on the flesh of a strawberry.

"Fuck," she whined.

She whipped out her phone in search of remedies. The cabinets were void of all but the basics. No toner or acne patches. Not even creams, which she admitted she hadn't purchased in years either. Scrolling told her to use rubbing alcohol and toothpaste, but she had doubts.

Then a notification popped up. RandysGurl (triple heart emoji) had posted again. Lizette tapped her screen, and the smiling faces of her ex-husband and the other woman appeared. Her ex was exactly how she expected him to be, with stray gray hairs and creases along his forward. But the dewy, smooth canvas of his lover's face, even as she smiled wide enough to show teeth, caught Lizette off guard. Among the hashtags was one that said *No Filter*. She zoomed in until she couldn't anymore, searching for an imperfection or enlarged pore.

"Liz? I gotta go, honey," Dot shouted.

Lizette exited the app and clicked off her screen and whispered "Fuck" again.

Dot was already standing at the door, her purse hanging from her shoulder.

"You sure you don't want to stay and watch a movie?" Lizette asked.

Dot leaned in for a hug but stopped short and grabbed Lizette's face between her hands. She said nothing for several minutes, her eyes fixated on the zit. Lizette gulped.

"Maybe ice it?" Dot muttered. "There's ice in the freezer."

"Ugh, so it *is* obvious." Lizette pulled away and frowned.

"Relax," Dot tsked. "That's what you came here to do anyway, right? A little ice, a few days of sunshine, and that thing will dry right up. In a week you'll forget you had it." She kissed her cheek. "Now enjoy your time. Call me if you need anything."

She sauntered off to her car.

Lizette grabbed ice cubes from the freezer and wrapped them in a paper towel then sat on the loveseat. As she pressed the ice against her chin, she felt the sting of the cold. She pulled out her phone and lit the screen again with the fuzzy, magnified skin of her ex-husband's lover. She scrolled through stills of bikini photos in the tropical sunshine, tight-laced corset dresses hugging an hourglass figure, a naked torso without a face but filled with lush, reflective locks and the flesh of her back as smooth and unblemished as a freshly printed magazine cover. No filter. No filter. No filter. Sometimes her ex-husband's face would pop into the feed and ruin the seamlessness of the experience. Lizette would scroll past him quickly, like winding through a commercial break, in order to obsess on her parts again—the curve of a breast, a tendril of hair, the sheen of a single fingernail—until it was well past midnight.

In the dark living room, a slow, incessant tap beat against the sliding glass doors.

"Go away!" Lizette shouted.

It didn't stop but increased its speed, begging for her attention.

"I said go away," she hissed. She dropped the phone on the couch and stormed over to the door, only to find the deck was vacant and the moon gone.

Tap. Tap. Fat drops of rain flew at her face and splattered along the windowpane.

She pressed a hand to her chin to find the zit was tighter and harder, with blood throbbing beneath the surface. In the bathroom, she doused it with rubbing alcohol and tried to pick gently at the grain of sand. But when it refused to budge, she suffocated it with a glob of stinging mint toothpaste and finished brushing her teeth.

"I need to go to bed," she said drearily and fell onto the pillow with the doctored side of her face upward. But her eyes transfixed on the endless feed of photos until exhaustion took over.

The next morning, bright sunshine pierced through the flamingo-printed curtains, along with a warm breeze. Her window was ajar, and the sound of rhythmic waves and cries of seagulls greeted her. Her head ached, not only from too much Moscato but because she'd rolled over and slept with her chin pressed against her phone. A smear of toothpaste covered its surface. When she lifted a hand to her jawline, she felt a dime-sized bump, angry and gnawing with needle-like pinches.

She shuffled to the bathroom and reached for the rubbing alcohol that had been left out on the countertop the night before. She doused a cotton ball in the pungent, clear liquid then pressed it against her face until the skin went numb. "Enough of that," she told her reflection in the mirror. "Enough."

She plated one of the pastries Dot left for her and drank coffee on the deck, away from her phone. She swore to abstain from the phone for the rest of the day, blaming the ballooning zit and her exhaustion on it. Instead, she'd throw some books and magazines into a beach bag and enjoy the sunshine, as Dot had recommended. She slipped on a one-piece and sarong and headed through the tall beach grass along the boardwalk toward the surf.

It was a picture-perfect day with no one in sight. There weren't even boats bobbing along the crystal blue waves. She trekked over thick, soft hills of sand until she reached the brim of the shoreline. Seashell fragments threatened each step beyond this line, so she planted her beach chair at the waterfront and kicked off her flip-flops.

The ocean waves stretched toward her with foamy lips. Her toes sank into the sand as bath-like water pooled around them. She audibly sighed and thought of how her ex-husband hated the beach, how he complained about the little grains of sand following you everywhere and the heat that never brought relaxation. But she could. Back in her youth, every summer, her parents would rent a cottage at the beach, just like Dot's, and Lizette would slather herself in baby oil and iodine to get the perfect, dark glow. That was how Randy had met her, on a beach, tanning in a tiny bikini. Given the Instagram account, she figured that's how he must have met her, too.

In her bag was a thermos with the rest of the bottle of Moscato from the previous night. She chugged in the cool sweetness as she unfolded a book she'd stolen off the "Take one, leave one" shelf at the cottage, although she realized her choice, a self-help book about divorce, was a bit masochistic. After one chapter, she put the book aside and succumbed to the buzz of wine and midday heat like old times. The zit throbbed against her face, flush with rubbing alcohol and fresh, circulating blood.

She tilted back her head and closed her eyes so she could doze while the sun fried the spot.

Before long though, she heard something splashing in the water nearby. She glanced up, expecting to see a bird or fish, but saw an old, impossibly tawny man in a speedo walking toward her. Lizette averted her eyes, hoping he'd simply pass by. But his loud, splashing footsteps approached and stopped beside her.

"Hey," he said.

Lizette frowned then slowly turned toward the man. His forehead was wrinkled and sweaty. Bursts of wiry gray hair sprung from his chest, and between his flaccid pecks was a long, pale scar. *Not this one. Any guy but this one*, she silently begged fate.

"Do you have sunscreen on?" he asked. "You should really wear more sunscreen."

Lizette squinted in disbelief. "Excuse me?"

"Sunscreen!" he insisted, gesturing with his hands for emphasis. "You know? It prevents wrinkles, and you're so pale, so pale you're going to burn without it. You're burning now."

Liz glanced down at her shoulders, where pink blushed the surface of her skin. She chuckled uncomfortably.

He leaned forward, fingers poised as if he were about to flick something from her face. "You seem to have got something there." His voice trailed off as he inched closer.

Lizette pulled back and waved her hands frantically between her face and the strange man. "I'm trying to enjoy the beach!" she yelled. "Fuck off!"

She prepared for violence, thinking he might explode into a verbal tirade or that he'd try to touch her again and she'd have to knock him out. But he shrugged and circumnavigated her, kicking the water with each step along the beach.

She tried to get comfortable again but couldn't manage it. Disappointed and perturbed, she collected her things and headed back through the tall grass that hid the cottage from view. Inside the bathroom, she examined every pore of her skin with disgust. They'd been getting bigger as she aged. No wonder one of them clogged and festered with such a nasty zit, she thought. And this weather, the humidity. It was all a perfect storm.

The news warned of more lightning along the coast that afternoon, so Lizette stayed put in the cottage and browsed through magazines left on the bookshelves by earlier renters. The covers were mostly young celebrities with textual promises dancing around their heads. *Flat abs now! Best sex of your life!* Every woman's tresses were fan-blown, and every inch of skin that could show was showing.

Her eyes landed on one tagline: *Gorgeous skin overnight!* She flipped pages to find the article. It offered little except a list of expensive over-the-counter products. Lizette closed the glossy and went to the bathroom again, alarmed by how much the zit had grown. It appeared to be taking over her jawline and creeping toward her lips. She wondered if it wasn't a zit after all but an ingrown hair or tumor, something a doctor should examine. But the grain of sand still stuck to the top, even sunk into the flesh as it threatened to grow around it. She wanted to pop it so badly.

She spent the next hour searching magazines for articles about at-home beauty treatments until she settled on a honey, lemon, and baking soda mask—things that she could find on the cottage's kitchen shelves. The lemon stung when she swiped the mask over her chin, covering the tender flesh she'd already exposed to the sun. But she sat and waited and just before the pain grew unbearable, she grabbed her phone and opened up RandysGurl triple heart emoji's feed. She scrolled until her face went numb.

In the morning, Lizette was pleased to feel the softness of her skin upon waking. But the mirror told another, nightmarish story, one where the zit had overtaken her lower chin, her right cheek bulging. The swelling pulled one side of her lip taut, as if she were smirking, and threatened to pop with each touch of her fingertips. The skin around the grain of sand was darker and flaking, teeming with stagnant blood beneath the enlarged pores, while the bulbous extremities were paler than her own skin.

She pulled a pair of nail trimmers from the bathroom drawer and held them against her face. The metal was so cool against the heat of her cheek. She considered drawing its sharp edge along the surface, peeling back the epidermis until blood and pus spilled out, until she squeezed it clean. But she hesitated.

Her phone chimed. Another post from RandysGurl triple heart emoji. This time it was a video titled "Salt Water." But Lizette couldn't even get the phone to unlock at the sight of her face. Her image was too distorted to recognize. Frustrated, she cursed as she keyed in the passcode.

Her ex-husband's lover greeted her with a smile and a perfectly framed glowing face, then she spoke for less than 30 seconds about her nightly regimen.

"Hey, lovelies! Here's my beauty tip for the day. Mix water and sea salt until it's the consistency of salt water. You know, like at the beach?" She paused here to laugh at herself. "Then I spritz it on my face every night before bed. See?" She pulled the lens closer to her skin and traveled up and down her cheeks. "I'm about to start my period, but it's as clear as can be. Just try it, and let me know if it works for you, too. Catch you next time, lovelies!"

Lizette wished she felt that *lovely*. She wished skin care made her laugh. Outside the bathroom window, the sound of crashing waves beckoned. Lizette thought of the throbbing sore on half her face and the advice, the salt water so close. She'd sunbathed yesterday, and it only made it worse. Maybe what she should have done was swim.

She threw on a muumuu and headed for the beach, glancing in both directions along the shore as she emerged from the beach grass. She'd be devastated if anyone saw her face with the growth overtaking it.

The sparkling water beckoned, and she waded in to her waist then squatted down to dunk her head. Yes, it stung against her cheek, but perhaps that meant it was working. Perhaps she'd finally find some relief.

She buried her face below the waves repeatedly, trying to hold her breath as long as she could, resisting the urge to scratch each time the salt tingled and burned.

When she resurfaced the last time, the man was standing at the shore, staring at her.

"I thought you were a bird until I got closer," he said matter-of-factly.

She noticed he had some cysts of his own, pockmarking each side of the scar that cleaved his chest. Some of them had burst already, like tiny, oozing boils. *Gross*, she thought and said, "Do you, like, live around here or something?"

He shook his head no. "Off season. Same with you?"

She harrumphed and pulled wet strands of hair away from

her eyes. "I told you to leave me alone yesterday. I haven't changed my mind."

He jumped back and let out a gasp. Then he pointed at her.

Lizette glanced behind her, thinking there might be a shark, then jumped frantically as she circled herself. The heavy, wet muumuu dragged behind her.

"What? What is it?" she screamed.

"Your face!" he shouted. "Holy Christ. Did you get stung by a stingray? We need to get you an ambulance. Help! Help!" he called to no one.

Lizette glared at him and sloshed out of the water. "*You're* the one who needs help," she chastised, covering half of her face with her hand. "Stalking women at the beach. Making fun of their appearance. Now get! If I see you around my cottage one more time, I'll call the cops." He stared with his mouth hanging open. "Get!" she screamed louder.

The man turned and walked back in the opposite direction, careful not to glance over his shoulder or slow his pace.

"Good," Lizette hissed.

She felt hot with anger from the insult, which only made the throbbing cyst throb more. When her hand lit against her cheek, she found the sand speck with her fingers, dug in her nail, and picked it out of the tender skin. She felt a rush of relief, then one of nausea. Just before she reached the beach grass divide, she bent over and tried to catch her breath. Something wasn't right, she realized. A seething pain crawled along her skull and down into her neck.

She shuffled slowly past the grass and onto the boardwalk, the beach house just out of sight. Then the skin of her face cracked open like an egg. She watched a thick stream of pus shoot across the boardwalk. Globs of skin and blood fell at her feet. Her skin ripped slowly down her shoulders and arms, chunks of flesh peeling back then slipping off in wet, sticky mounds. Her lips parted into a terrified scream then pulled back and wide. Two soft, red lips surfaced from the zit and parted with a deep, moaning sound. They continued moaning as the rest of Lizette's skin fell like a jacket to reveal another body.

Lizette glanced down at her figure, so lean and tawny. So remarkably smooth beneath the remaining streaks of blood. She wiped off the blood and noticed a slim bikini tied against her taut hip bones and full breasts. Then she walked her hands up to her face, where they were met with lean, high cheekbones and a tapered jaw. She felt no disfiguration, no burning, not even a tingle.

Footsteps tiptoed on the boardwalk behind her. She turned and caught a young man staring at her.

"I thought I heard a scream back here," he said.

They both glanced down at the pile of crumbled flesh around her feet then up at the dribbles of blood running down her legs.

She fiddled with her hair and said, "Oh, that was me. I didn't think anyone was around to hear it."

The young man kept staring at her intently. His hair was wavy, thick, and sun streaked. He was so muscular and tan. Just as tan as her, except for one faint line that ran down his chest. A pale scar, the only flaw on his entire body. At his ankles were tendrils of body tissue, still sanguine on one side.

She smiled and he smiled back, their matching white teeth glistening. Then she lowered her eyes shyly.

"Hey, lovely," he said, taking her by the hand. "Want to take a walk with me?"

She nodded, and together they strolled back to the shore,

leaving a Lizette-shaped puddle to shrivel in the sun.

147

End of Day

Margo stood outside of Products 2 People's main office, swiping her badge repeatedly. A small red light stared up at her, and down the street, an unseasonal Florida storm crept closer. She worried she would be stranded when it arrived. It was still much too early to wait for help. Behind the branded glass front doors, the security guard desk was empty, and the Christmas tree was off. Normally, the tree was lit day and night for the entire last quarter. Orange in October. Black lights on Black Friday. Blue and white for Hanukkah. But today, the start of the week before Christmas, it was as if everyone was on vacation but her.

She swiped again, and the panel light finally turned green. The door released, and Margo made her way past the vacant cubicles toward a locked room, where her team evaluated jewelry samples.

When Margo was onboarded, she was told most of what she evaluated should be in the clear. But through diligence or luck, she'd found the fakes—vermeil passed off as gold, undisclosed treatments, and dyes. Her discoveries saved P2P's revenue and reputation more than once, so the department bestowed her with an award. Because the ceremony coincided with the same day a new management position opened, Margo believed she was a shoo-in for the promotion. Arriving early and leaving late as they conducted interviews would prove that to her boss, Gail.

She filled her coffee mug and settled into her seat, then turned on her computer. An email from Gail appeared around 8:30 a.m.

I'll need your report by end of day.

Margo wondered what this meant. Outside, the sky was almost black with the slow-approaching storm. She finished a few tasks then headed to Gail's office but found it empty and locked. So she returned to the jewelry room, where her coworkers were chatting.

"Did you see how empty it was out there this morning?" Nancy asked. Nancy had promised to show up in ugly Christmas sweaters all week. Today a very fat cat wedged into a brick chimney was stamped on her chest. "'Twas the week before Christmas and all through the office, not a creature was stirring, not even a—"

"Manager," Andrea hissed. "A manager. Has anyone seen Gail? I was supposed to have a touch base with her at 8:30 a.m."

Margo was about to say she'd already checked Gail's office, but then she heard Andrea's fervent typing.

Typical Gail. She always ran late—hadn't even been on time for Margo's first interview. But Gail's poor sense of timing also meant Margo could saunter in late and still seem right on time.

Typical Andrea, too. She'd waste her morning drafting hate emails, then complain that she didn't have enough time to finish her work. The team knew better than to argue with Andrea, though. Year after year, Andrea survived P2P's annual 'holiday layoffs.' A local business magazine had coined the term because P2P layoffs were always wedged between Thanksgiving and Christmas, filling every employee's stocking with dread.

They believed this was because Andrea once threatened P2P with legal action over a parking spot. Next thing they knew, she was getting not only designated space near the front, but extra PTO, long lunches, and a flexible work schedule.

Still, Margo chocked up Andrea's immunity to the layoffs to her seniority at the company. It was simple corporate mathematics. She could get away with murder because, with her experience, perks were cheaper than funding the search for someone new. Margo herself had survived her second layoff season with more confidence that she would survive the next.

Her coworker Nancy started humming Christmas tunes, popping bubblegum while examining product at her desk.

"Too early for breakfast bubblegum, Nance," Andrea huffed. "I can't hear myself think." She continued her furious typing.

Margo watched as Nancy walked over to the shared trashcan and spit out her gum. It was sad. Nancy was a gentle, trusting soul, and all the life had been beaten out of her by the corporate stick.

Tina, the youngest of the group but still more senior at the company than Margo, came around the corner with a tray of jewelry samples. Margo glanced up.

"Killer heels!" Tina said, pointing at the floor.

A pair of red stilettos with a covered toe and ankle strap peeked out from Margo's dress pants. Margo smiled. "They're ours. Or were," she said. "Employee discount and Christmas gift to myself. Now they're sold out."

Tina smirked. "You lucky bitch."

Margo was drawn to Tina first for her keen fashion sense, not to mention her wit. Today, a green sheath draped along her curvy silhouette, and a fancy pattern danced through her black pantyhose. She looked librarian smart in her glasses, but what had sealed the friendship was Tina's mouth. Two perfectly painted red lines that sometimes framed the most inappropriate language.

Margo returned to her computer screen and the email from her manager.

She started typing *I'm not sure what you mean.* Then lightning struck and the lights flickered out. Nancy gasped, and the sound of Tina dropping her tray of jewelry echoed throughout the room. A long drawl of thunder vibrated the windows.

"Everyone okay?" Nancy asked through the darkness.

"Stupid storm," Tina moaned. "I'm fine, but I just dropped my entire fucking sample tray. If a diamond rolled into hiding, I'm screwed. Forget Christmas bonus. How about a Christmas deduction?"

The wind outside strengthened, and tree branches scratched across the glass. But Margo was sold on the idea that this was the safest room at the company. The windows were polycarbonate—burglar-proof and impossible to break, which made sense for a room with hundreds of thousands of dollars' worth of fine jewelry. The only true concerns that ever crossed Margo's mind were fires or broken air conditioning units. She remembered the latter as the heat crept in, perspiration forming above her upper lip.

"It's too bloody hot in here for a sweater now," Nancy complained. "Hope no one has to see me naked."

Margo cringed. Classic Nancy. It wasn't what she shared that bothered the team, but how she shared it. She often took personal calls at her desk. Everyone already knew her ex-husband drained their bank account before he left and, more recently, she had some sort of fungal infection that concerned her doctor.

Pale emergency lights in each corner of the room flickered on, along with their computer screens again. They all breathed a collective sigh of relief.

"Finally, bathroom time," Nancy chirped. "That lightning scared the piss out of me."

Nancy's kitten heels thudded along the thin carpet toward the door. She swiped her badge once, then twice, then paused.

"Um, I think it's still locked," Nancy announced to the room.

Andrea stood. "That's impossible. The doors activate when the emergency lights kick in. It's a safety protocol."

"Can you try your badge then, Andrea?"

Andrea huffed and marched over to the door, swiped her badge once, then twice, then paused and glanced nervously at Nancy. "I'll call security."

By the time Andrea made it back to her desk and picked up her phone, Margo and Tina were also taking turns swiping their badges. A red light as persistent as Rudolph's nose stared back at them.

Andrea cursed and slammed down the phone. "Apparently the phones don't restart when we're on backup power." She turned to Nancy. "You'll just have to hold it until we get out of here. I don't get paid enough to watch my coworkers pee in cups."

Nancy frowned and went knock-kneed. "Well, I hope it's soon. My bladder isn't what it used to be, and it's getting too hot in here to wear a Christmas sweater." The sagging fat cat on her chest seemed to agree.

"I'll email them," Margo offered calmly. "After all, the computers came back on."

She returned to her desk and opened her inbox, minimizing the draft of her response to Gail's message. It was well past 10 a.m., but one couldn't tell by looking out the darkened windows.

Margo opened a new email addressed to P2PSecurity, typed a quick message about the door, and CC'ed Gail. Then she pressed send. "Done. We should hear back from them soon."

Another round of lightning crackled outside, and a shadow materialized from one of the abandoned cubicles at the end of the row. "They aren't coming," a voice whispered. The entire team jumped.

It was Claire, a copywriter from a neighboring department. She was one of the few writers with access to the evaluation room because she wrote marketing copy for jewelry.

"Jesus Christ, Claire," Nancy wailed. "You scared us. How long have you been in here?"

Claire stepped from around the corner with her hands folded at her waist. "I don't know. I needed to grab a sample because the photos on the evaluation were hard to make out."

Andrea harrumphed. "I told you a week ago that brand was moved to these containers over here." She pointed to a shelf beside her. "And I've never let an eval pass with bad photos."

"Give her a break, Andrea," Tina said. "She's stuck in a hot, locked room because of your—"

Margo interrupted. "Wait. What do you mean they're not coming, Claire?"

Claire cleared her throat. "You know that ding sound the computer makes when an email is bounced back?" She pointed at Margo's computer. "See for yourself."

Everyone rushed to Margo's desk. Her inbox contained one message:

MAILER-DAEMON. We're sorry to inform you that your message could not be delivered to one or more of the following recipients

attached below. But have an awesome day!
  Security@P2P.com

"That's the correct address," Nancy sighed over Margo's shoulder. "I wish I'd passed on coffee this morning. Perhaps we can knock on the door until someone hears us."

Nancy and Tina pounded on the door and shouted at the tiny window above their heads. When they tired, Claire and Andrea threw their fists against it, too.

Margo remembered the empty rows of cubicles she passed this morning. Cubicles that would be deserted throughout the day, even as she passed for coffee, lunch, or a quick walk. She made her way back to her desk and slipped off her heels. Then she got to working typing an email with everyone she knew CC'ed, even external vendors. All quickly returned, ding after ding.

"I can't get a message to anyone."

Then another email from Gail appeared. The same message from this morning, word-for-word, but with a different time stamp. *I'll need your report by end of day.*

Margo wondered how Gail was able to get email in when she couldn't send anything out. Perhaps the second email was a glitch or a pre-scheduled message caught in a loop.

By the time Margo gave up and returned to the group in her bare feet, Nancy was breathless and sweaty. The sleeves of her sweater were bunched up to her elbows. "There has to be something we can do."

Tina also had sweat stains blooming from her armpits. She slipped behind a cubicle wall and removed her tights. "So much better," she said as she reemerged.

But there was a wild look in Andrea's eyes. The heat was

getting to her. Her face reddened as she glanced around at each of them, then she stormed back to her desk. "If you all would have just backed me when I told Gail that we needed to keep this door unlocked in case of an emergency, this never would have happened!"

Margo glanced at Tina, neither knowing what to make of it. "We didn't know you wanted that, Andrea," Tina called down the row.

"Sure. So that must be why you all chose to discuss it when I was on vacation. She said you unanimously voted it down."

Nancy huddled closer to Claire, Tina, and Margo. "Do you know what the hell she's talking about now?" Nancy whispered.

"I'm not even on your team. All I wanted was a sample," Claire whispered back.

Tina rolled her eyes. "You know how she gets. Blaming everyone but herself."

"I heard that!" Andrea shouted.

Something flew at them. Margo ducked just as the lights died again. She heard a loud thud, then one of her coworkers moaned.

"God dammit, Andrea! You're out of control," Tina yelled through the dark.

Margo bent to the floor, toward the sound of shallow breathing. Her hands felt along the floor until she grasped hair between her fingers. Something sticky. Lighting flashed across the sky as she lifted her hands. At her feet was Nancy's head. Dark red blood crawling toward Margo's bare feet. Blood dripped from her hand onto Nancy's cold, pale face.

The emergency lights appeared as small halos in each corner of the room, even dimmer than before. Margo shook Nancy's shoulders, but she wouldn't respond.

"What do we do? What do we do?" Claire shouted.

"We need to stop the blood," Margo insisted.

Tina grabbed her tights from the nearby desk as Margo propped up Nancy's head onto her lap. On her left temple, a gash peeled back to expose pink flesh beneath blonde hair. They wrapped the tights around Nancy's crown a few times and tied a knot. Then they waited. Nancy felt like dead weight in Margo's arms. She clutched Nancy's wrist between her fingers and felt nothing.

That's when she and Tina spotted the stapler, smeared with blood, on the carpet.

Andrea rounded the corner and spotted them. "It was meant for Tina. So you all can blame her."

Tina and Andrea argued as Claire wandered off toward the polycarbonate windows. Her voice quivered. "Guys? There's something out there."

She dropped to her knees and crawled quickly back toward the group, as if she were hiding.

"Have you gone mad?" Andrea scolded.

Claire wriggled in between them. When she glanced up, her teeth were chattering. Sweat matted her hair to her forehead. "S-s-someone in a black raincoat. Outside the window. But his face . . ." she sobbed. "There was no f-f-face. We have to get out of here!"

Tina shushed her. "Now, Claire, we're not going to let anyone hurt you. Come here." Claire buried herself in Tina's arms, and Tina gave Margo a look over her shoulder. "If we can't get out in this storm, then no one's trying to get in. Yet! We can't get out *yet*." She laughed uncomfortably. "We just need to wait until someone can open this door." She turned to Margo and mouthed "do something."

A shadow passed outside the door. Claire noticed and freed herself of Tina's arms and punched the small, reinforced window until Margo thought she'd break her knuckles.

"Come back!" Claire wailed. "Come back! We're trapped in here!"

Tina grabbed Margo by the hand and led her back to her desk. "We have to figure something out. What about your cell phone?"

"I always lose the signal when it's stormy," said Margo.

"Yeah. Mine's dead because we can't fucking charge anything without power." She craned her neck. "Claire? Andrea?" Claire stopped pounding at the door. "Either of your cell phones work right now?"

"No signal," said Andrea.

"Mine's still at my desk. In the other room. Out there," Claire said longingly.

Margo pulled at Tina's arm and lowered her voice. "Nancy's dead. I felt her wrist before Claire wandered off. No pulse."

Tina blinked at her. "I'm going to get us out of here," she whispered back. "Then I'm going to kill Andrea with my bare hands."

Tina searched for a screwdriver and exclaimed when she found one in her box of tools. She marched over to the door and told Claire to stand back. "We'll be out of here in no time!" she said, pressing the tip into one of the bottom hinge screw heads.

Claire wandered back over to the window, and Margo followed her. Outside, the rain fell in sheets. They could make out the walkway that hugged the building, but not the parking spaces, street, or other buildings beyond it.

Claire shook as she spoke. "He was here, you know. I'm not crazy. I just—"

A figure lurched toward the window. Black raincoat, shadowed hood. It must have been at least seven feet tall. The whole body slammed into the windowpane until it cracked.

It cracked. They told us that couldn't happen, Margo thought.

Claire backed into Margo, who backed into a desk chair. The two were like sheets of paper stapled together. Broken glass cascaded into the room as the dark figure's arms lunged forward and plucked up Claire. She grasped onto Margo's hands as she was pulled, flailing and screaming. The rain washed in and pelted Margo's face. She could feel her grip loosening. Then Claire relaxed her fingertips and went limp.

"Margo?" she whispered.

Blood began to trickle from the corner of her mouth. She went motionless, like a rag doll hanging over the window frame. Margo covered her mouth. Upright shards of glass, still attached to the windowsill, had caught Claire's torso. Blood dripped down the wall onto the carpet and mixed with rain. Margo's hands began to shake.

The last thing she remembered was Tina pulling her back from the window and her own voice screaming.

* * *

"Wake up, Margo. Wake up."

Andrea swatted Margo's cheeks until she opened her eyes. They were on the other side of the row of cubicles, as far away from the broken window as they could be.

Margo's clothes were drenched and wet against her skin. "Claire was right. She—"

She felt Andrea's grip tighten. "Hush. Shhh. Tina's working on the door hinges. We still need to get out of here."

The power surged and the lights brightened momentarily.

Margo stood and ran over to her desk. "Maybe the email will work now," she said. "It's our only hope." Dozens of copies of Gail's message now filled her inbox. She opened one of them and wrote: *Claire and Nancy dead. Send help!*

She pressed 'Send' and drummed her fingers while she waited.

Andrea appeared beside her. "You didn't tell us Gail was messaging you."

"I can get emails but not send them. Remember? That message was from earlier this morning. It's like the system keeps sending it again." She minimized her screen.

"Interesting," Andrea replied. "I guess all we can do is wait. Right? Tina, how's it going over there?"

Tina stood on a chair, working on the uppermost door hinge while screws littered the floor. "Almost got it. I just need to—" Tina's chair tilted as the door wobbled backward. As she tried to steady it again, she gazed through the small window. Her lower jaw dropped, and her eyes widened. "It's that thing! What Claire saw! It's trying to get inside. Help me!"

Andrea and Margo ran toward her and caught the weight of the door as it fell. A hungry, ravenous scream pierced the air, and several hands reached around the door. They pushed and pulled at everything they touched. Margo didn't know how much longer she could last.

Tina stabbed one of the hands with a pencil. "Stop it!" she squealed.

The hand latched onto her wrist and pulled her body between the heavy door and frame.

Her face began to turn purple. "It hurts," she gasped.

Then she vanished. The door collapsed on Margo and Andrea, and they heard Tina's screams echo down the hallway.

Once Margo freed herself, she tried to figure out what to do. Andrea had disappeared, and when she walked around the row of cubicles to find her, Andrea was at the other end, breathing heavily. A pair of scissors was poised above her head.

"Down to one!" Andrea screamed, a wild look overtaking her eyes.

"Andrea, what are you doing?"

Andrea ran toward Margo as lightning flashed and cut the lights again.

Margo dropped to the floor and skirted away from Andrea's path.

"Don't play dumb. You knew exactly why Gail sent us that email this morning, why Nancy's dead, why Tina's about to be. Only so many people can make it to the top, Margo." She could hear Andrea fumble in the dark, the snipping of the scissors in her hand. "The good news is it's down to us. The bad news is it's about to be just me."

Margo shuddered. She crept past Claire's limp body, beads of sweat running down her forehead. She tried not to gasp for air, but her heart pounded in her ears. Then the room was silent again. Margo slipped under one of the abandoned desks right before Andrea tiptoed past, and once she was far enough away, Margo bolted.

But Andrea was closer and faster than Margo predicted. She wouldn't make it to the door. She lunged for her cubicle and grasped one of her red high heels in her hands. She swung it over her shoulder just in time for the heel to catch Andrea's neck. Margo watched as the tender flesh caved in and Andrea stumbled forward.

"You bitch," Andrea sputtered. "I have seniority. I earned this."

She dropped the scissors. Blood cascaded onto her chest, and she braced herself down to the carpet. Indistinguishable curses slipped between her wet coughs until she finally was still.

Margo braced herself in her desk chair, and the power flickered on. All the computers and phones booted up, their sounds like knives cutting through the silence. An email chimed as it arrived in her inbox.

Please see me in my office. -Gail

Margo read it over and over again, unsure what to think. She grabbed her purse and wiped her nose with a tissue, then hobbled around Andrea's corpse. Margo didn't know how she would explain her missing shoes, the blood, the bodies. She clutched her badge and peeked around the door frame, expecting a hooded creature to grab her. But there was no one. Just florescent lights lining the hallway. The soft touch of air conditioning cooled her brow.

She limped toward Gail's office and waited at the door until Gail gestured for her to come in. Then she took a seat across from Gail. Two men, dressed in suits and seated in a corner, were waiting in the office as well. They stared at Margo as she wiped sweat from her face and cleared her throat. She wondered if they were police.

Gail leaned forward and folded her hands together. She had a smile on her face. "So, first of all, congratulations. You got the promotion."

Margo gulped.

"All those reports you sent me today were exactly what we needed." Gail turned toward the men, and they all shook heads approvingly.

Margo glanced between them. "I thought the email system was down."

"Well, you're a promising young woman, Margo. I knew that the moment I hired you that you could do it."

Margo tried to speak, to explain the terror, the mad look in Andrea's eyes. But she couldn't help but notice her manager's persistent smile. When she peered back at the two men again, she spotted the black, hooded capes folded beneath their chairs.

"Your new role starts tomorrow," Gail continued. "Of course, your first task will be hiring a new team now that your old one is . . . terminated." The men and Gail shared a long laugh that made Margo's left eye twitch. "So take the rest of the week off. After all, it's the holidays. We know you'll make P2P proud."

Margo nodded her head and peeled herself from the chair. She staggered down the hallway toward the security desk. Outside, the sun was finally emerging. Margo stepped into its light. And she ran, as far and as fast as she could, her badge falling behind her.

Tourniquet

Ilia wakes to another woman's screams at the end of the cell block. But the sound is softer than she expects from someone waking from a nightmare. Instead, the screams are bloodless, meandering, as if the woman is getting pulled down a drain, deeper into the guts of the prison. When the voice is snuffed out by the sound of a slamming door, the silence that follows is so pervasive it makes Ilia's throat tighten.

She sits erect in her bunk. Above her, Willow, her cellmate, still sleeps. A skinny flashlight beam appears, and a shadowed figure approaches the bars of their cell.

"Psst," the shadow whispers. "Halls. Your turn. Get a move-on."

Handcuffs catch the light.

"Right now?" She sighs, exasperated. "It's the middle of the night."

The guard narrows his gaze. "Did I stutter?"

Ilia frowns and lowers her gaze. She feels around the floor for her shoes, finds them, and ties the laces slowly. *No matter what they say, no matter what they do, don't resort to violence,* her brain repeats.

Every day she has to remind herself. Violence got her here. Violence against a man, who used violence against her first. But no one was there to see the struggle. He choked her, she told the jury, so she stabbed him. A dozen times. She'd been running on adrenaline and the fear that he'd get up and try it again.

The guard beats his baton against the bars. "Up. Now," he instructs.

Ilia stands and lets the guard cuff her hands behind her and leads her down the row, where she's escorted through two locked doors into an examination room that reeks of antiseptic. The nurse is new, but a dead-ringer for the ones before her. The doctor has a type, Ilia realizes. Blonde. Curvaceous. Obedient. She instructs Ilia to take a seat then signals the guard that he can leave. He rearranges Ilia's cuffs to the front so she can sit. She stays as still as possible, so he won't get the wrong impression, like that one time she tried to scratch her arm and the guard walloped her with his baton. She couldn't blame him, she told herself. He probably thought she was about to run for it.

Ilia blinks against the sharp fluorescent lights and maneuvers into the chair as he watches. He warns her not to run with his stare, then he turns to leave. She eyes the room while she waits: manila cupboards against manila walls, a sink, a thick folder clamped shut with a black binder clip. Ilia wonders what's written about her inside the file.

When the nurse bends over to gather some items from a drawer, Ilia spots a tattoo along her neck. A blue caduceus, with two snakes entwined around a staff, sits just above the collar. She's puzzled, but her curiosity is interrupted by the sound of Velcro ripping. The nurse wraps a blood pressure cuff around Ilia's right arm and presses a cold stethoscope against her skin. The nurse compliments the size of her veins, how easy the blood draw will be with a patient like her, as she pumps the bulb.

Already Ilia's sweating. The pressure builds, and she tries to inhale. But she's frozen. The veins in her arm compress, squeezing against muscle and bone. Her heart pounds through the arteries and into her eardrums, louder and louder. She feels the blood draining from her face. Then the tightness releases. Everything within her exhales.

"Blood pressure's a little high," the nurse remarks. When she lifts her gaze, she notices the beads glistening along Ilia's forehead. Her face is clammy and cold to the touch. "Blood scare you? Just look away, hon. We'll be done before you know it."

Ilia appreciates the nurse's kindness, but it's a foreign and strange feeling. She licks her lips, dry with anticipation. "Not blood," Ilia says breathily. "It's that." She points at the table beside her, at the blue band folded on itself next to an empty tube.

"The tourniquet?" she asks. Ilia nods her head. "Haven't heard that one before. You sure you're not afraid of blood?"

"No, ma'am. My older brother, he had a snake when we were kids. He'd wait until I was asleep, then he'd sneak into my room and let that thing curl itself around my arms and legs. I'd wake up screaming, which would only panic the snake and make it grip tighter.

"One time it bit me, and I felt like I couldn't breathe. They know better than to do it now, but my daddy wrapped his belt around my arm so tight it throbbed and swelled all the way to the hospital. He thought it would stop the venom from spreading, but it just made it worse. That's why I have this big, black mark on me." She nods her head backwards toward a bruise-like circle hidden under her sleeve.

The nurse blinks twice, speechless, and unsure what to say. She wants to tell the nurse about her husband and the time he choked her. When he did it, he lifted her up in the air while he gripped her throat, as she scrambled for the knife in her pocket, but she thinks better of it. No one here was hired to sympathize with her. She's already made it awkward enough, and it's never made a difference in what happens next.

The doctor enters the room unannounced and clears his throat. Ilia notices the intake of the nurse's breath, how her jaw clenches and her eyes widen.

"I'll be fast," she whispers to Ilia—or to the doctor. Ilia isn't sure. "Now make a fist like this."

Ilia mimics the locked elbow and tight fist of the nurse as best she can while cuffed. A moist alcohol wipe glides over the crook of her arm. She averts her gaze as the nurse wraps the tourniquet around her limb and knots it with a snap. Her eyes meet the doctor's as he glances up from reading the thick file on the countertop. He frowns at her, so she averts her eyes across the room toward the door.

A sound, like a far-off whistle, begins to fill Ilia's ears. She squirms a little as the needle is inserted, trying to keep the sweat from rolling into her eyes. The door and every surface around are cut by pinpricks of light.

"I—I hear it," Ilia moans. Her tongue feels fat inside her mouth.

"Hear what, sweetie?" The nurse's voice sounds like she's underwater.

Then everything goes dark.

* * *

Ilia wakes abruptly. She's back in prison cell 4C, and the pale pink light of dawn spills onto the floor. Willow's awake and tapping her shoulder until their eyes meet.

"Rise and shine. You missed the call for count. It's in ten minutes."

Ilia raises a hand to her skull. It hurts, like she slid out of the chair and hit her head on the floor of the infirmary. She releases the too-tight gauze wrapped around her arm and flexes her hand to get the blood circulating.

"Another blood draw?" Willow asks. "Your thyroid again?"

"I can only assume. It's my husband's fault. I never had a thyroid problem until he choked me."

"Well, I think you got him back for that one." Willow winks.

Ilia stands but feels wobbly and sits back down again.

"Not too fast," Willow whispers. "They had to carry you back this time. Just sit here with me until it passes."

Ilia reclines and wonders when the room will stop spinning. "I just feel so—so violated," she complains. "Every day of my life. Out there. In here." She gestures with her hands. "I went from one abusive relationship into another—with this damn place. They keep poking me and not saying why. Just giving or taking away pills. For all I know, I could have cancer."

Willow chuckles. "At least cancer would be a way out of here."

She nudges Ilia, who rolls onto her stomach, letting Willow brush her fingertips up and down her back until the room is still again. When they were first paired, Ilia didn't want a soul to touch her, not after what she'd been through. But Willow said the finger brushing thing helped calm her children when they felt sick. So Ilia let her try, and it did help.

This and finding out Willow was serving a life sentence for selling a few bags of pot to an undercover cop built trust and a bond between them. In spite of Ilia murdering her husband, Willow didn't seem concerned. She understood. They'd both been wronged by the system.

"You know I had that dream again," Willow says. "That one where we were running around out there on Halloween night, like kids in costumes. Free."

Ilia buries her face into the pillow. "Sometimes all I dream about is setting fire to this mattress then laying down in it."

"Girl, stop. You're my road dog, the only person here who keeps me sane. If we keep each other in check, they'll release us both for good behavior. It happens all the time."

Ilia stops herself from rolling her eyes. "Happens in the movies. Something tells me that's not going to happen here. The only parole they'll offer us is back door parole. In a body bag."

Willow pouts but doesn't counter her. "Go on with your pity party. I won't stop you. But it won't be contagious today. They're giving me this new drug for my depression. I'm not sure if it's working yet. We'll see. I do feel a little lighter, though. Maybe it's just this time of year." She glances over at the paper calendar stuck to the wall with tape, the one Willow brought from the previous prison. Three pumpkins, one large and two small, are drawn with pen on the 31st of October. "It's almost Halloween. You remember what it was like at the other prison?"

"Sure do," Ilia grins. "Decorating cards. Painting our faces. The guards would always pass out candy, and we'd dump it in a big pile so you moms could divide it into whose kid liked what."

The smile fades from Willow's face. "I miss my kids," she says softly. "I miss cutting eye holes in bed sheets and taking them to the rich kids' neighborhood, where it's safe to trick-or-treat. They're probably at my sister's house, saying trick-ortreating is stupid this year." She gives a half-hearted smile as a tear slips down her cheek. "They'll watch Halloween movies and eat all the candy they were supposed to pass out, just like I did at their age." She shakes her head.

Ilia rolls over and hugs her tight from behind, glancing down at Willow's forearms, where long, pale scars pucker the skin.

"I'm sorry about all of it," Ilia says. "Maybe we can do something to celebrate. Create some kind of distraction for ourselves."

"I bet candy's contraband here, like every other kind of joy," Willow says. "Look at me," she scoffs, "I just told you I wasn't going to catch your bad mood today, and here I am." She walks over to the bars and presses her forehead against the cold metal. "What did we do to get stuck in this place, Ilia? Where we can't even have visitors?"

Hushed voices rush past their cell. "Confirmed. Block C. Over," one of the correctional officers says. A few minutes later, medical staff rush past, too. Ilia remembers the screams from last night. She and Willow try to eavesdrop on the conversation, but it disappears down the row, in the direction of the Hole.

"I heard someone screaming from the Hole last night, just before they came to get me," Ilia says.

"I'd scream too if I was in the Hole," Willow whispers.

The count takes another hour to finish. Ilia's stomach growls. When they're released, the women are led directly to the yard instead of the chow hall. A correctional officer throws a cheese pastry at each one on their way through the doors.

Ilia watches as Willow separates from her and walks toward the high wall, as far away from watchful eyes as she can get, and bumps fists with another inmate before they exchange gossip.

Ilia devours the cheese pastry and sits down to watch. Some

inmates smoke. Some play basketball. Some run around the perimeter fence. Ilia likes to close her eyes and imagine she's somewhere else. When it's warm, she imagines she's at the beach. When it's cold, she imagines she's at a ski resort. She's never seen these places in real life, but she's read about them.

Eventually Willow's shadow appears over Ilia's shoulder. "I heard something about that scream," she says.

Ilia leans closer as Willow serves a play-by-play about an inmate, someone new, spitting in a correctional officer's face then being dragged to the Hole. She claims the woman hung herself in the middle of the night.

Ilia grabs her neck instinctively. She remembers her husband's hands around it, tightening until the last of her breath squeaked out. She knows she couldn't scream more than once. Neither would a woman hanging herself.

"Willow, everyone knows there's nothing in the Hole but four walls and a drain for pissing. What did she hang herself with?"

"Well, that's what everybody says about the Hole, but do we really know? Has anyone made it out of there to tell us?"

Ilia considers this and nods. "Who told you?"

Willow hesitates. "I don't usually share my source, but Tristan, the chick in the cell closest to the Hole, said so. She overheard the medical staff talking about it."

They both glance over at Tristan, until she catches them watching her. She makes a gesture with her finger across her neck at Willow. They glance back at each other and head in the opposite direction together.

When everyone is called back and lined up for a count, Ilia and Willow notice an intense stench just beyond the doors. A black body bag sits in the hallway with a still-wet, bloody handprint on top. Ilia wonders why there would be blood if last night's victim strangled herself. Then she wonders if it's a different inmate altogether. She scans the line in front and behind her, searching for a missing person, but she can't identify one.

When a guard screams that they should get to their work assignments instead of gawking, they scatter like animals running from a predator.

Ilia makes her way to the supply closet for her work assignment as an orderly, only to feel a shadow lurking at her back.

"Halls. We've got something for you to clean up." The guard curls his finger, beckoning her.

Ilia hesitates but knows she must follow, or she'll be in worse trouble later. *Don't resort to violence* she thinks as her grip tightens on the mop handle. The guard quickens his pace. He leads her to the body bag, now tucked into a private room near the entrance of the infirmary.

"I need you to grab something off of this while I, eh, go for a stroll." He winks. "Then clean up the handprint before the coroner gets here."

"This? You mean the body?" she asks. "What do you want me to get?"

"Necklace. Leave it in the grate by the janitor's closet when you're done. And Halls?" He leans forward until his nose almost touches hers. She can smell his acrid breath. "If you say anything about this, I'll kill you."

He turns and walks away.

Ilia props the mop handle against the wall. When she glances around, no one is watching. She doesn't hear any footsteps down the hall. She inhales into her sleeve and unzips the bag.

Matted, disheveled blonde hair materializes first. The face is turned away. But she notices the head is large and somewhat swollen, each fiber of hair taut in its shaft. She wonders what kind of beating the woman had to suffer to swell this much.

She opens the zipper farther down and stops at the collar bone. The neck is bruised. Dotted in blue ink along the skin is the blue caduceus, with two serpents entwined around a staff.

She recoils and hunches over, feeling like she might vomit, but she doesn't. Her mind spins from the nurse at her blood draw to the scream from last night and how they couldn't be the same person. The timing is all wrong. She reaches out her hand to feel for the necklace. The skin is cool to the touch everywhere. She finds it, fumbling with the clasp until it finally gives. Then she quickly zips up the bag, wipes away the handprint, and bolts for the supply closet.

Back at the supply closet, the necklace dangles from her fingertips over the drain in the floor. It's just a gold chain, she thinks, thick and slippery like a snake. She wonders if the guard wants to sell it, melt it down for cash, give it to someone else in the prison as a favor or payment, or for sentimental reasons. Maybe he and the nurse had an affair. Maybe he tried to strangle her too, and he got away with it. Whatever happens to it, she wants nothing to do with it. She releases her grip, and the necklace clinks softly, metal against metal, before it slithers between the teeth of the grate.

Her appetite evaporates by the end of her work assignment. No matter how much shit she scrubs away, she can't purge the bloated head and tattoo from her mind. She bypasses the chow hall and heads back to her cell at 4C, determined to lose herself in a book.

It's silent for a while, then the inmates start returning from their meal. But it's another hour before Willow appears. When she does, she's cupping water in one hand and holding something against her face with the other. It's an ice cube bleeding through a paper towel. She pulls it away from her mouth to reveal a scab covering one side of her lower lip.

"What happened to you?" Ilia exclaims.

The lip is inflamed and puffy and pulls to one side as Willow speaks. "Apparently Tristan didn't like me telling everybody what she overheard this morning. She said I was gonna get her in trouble with the guards. Didn't think about that. I guess I don't blame her."

"So she just cold-cocked you in the chow line?"

"Pretty much. Dinner and a show, right? Bitch got pepper sprayed after she did it, though." Willow sets the water down on the desk.

"Did they write you up?" Ilia asks.

"Not yet. They sent me straight to the infirmary. Well, the kitchen staff did. The guards didn't give a fuck. They would've let her shiv me." She puts the ice cube to her inflamed lip again. "No stitches needed, though. Painkillers, yes. They even squeaked in another round of my treatment while I was there."

"I just worry," Ilia admits. "What if they put something in your record? What about getting out of here together?"

"Don't worry, girl. I didn't throw the punches. I just took them."

Ilia wants to tell Willow what happened, about the body bag and the tattoo and the necklace the guard instructed her to hide. But she worries if she tells Willow she'll let that detail slip at the wrong time, too. Then infractions on their records will be the least of their worries.

The light fades from the afternoon and darkens the row. The guards go through their final count and dim the lights. Ilia turns on her lamp and reads.

"Read me a story," Willow says, "so I can fall asleep."

Ilia remembers when Willow first joined her in a cell at the earlier prison. They bonded over broken sleep and bright lights that were illuminated most of the night there. Ilia had never slept well outside of prison anyway but found reading was a gateway when it did happen. So whenever Willow found herself unable to sleep or up after another nightmare, Ilia would read to her.

"Sure." Ilia replies. "Tonight it's *Their Eyes Were Watching God*, just before the hurricane."

"My favorite," Willow says.

Ilia's soothing voice drifts up into Willow's ears until she hears Willow's soft snoring between sentences. She dog-ears the book and slips it under her pillow and turns out the light.

* * *

In the middle of the night, another noise startles Ilia. At their bars stand two correctional officers, their faces hidden in shadow.

"That's her," one of them says. He points his flashlight toward Willow in the top bunk.

Shit, Ilia thinks. She scampers up. Willow's mattress squeaks as well. The flashlight beam tilts downward, and Ilia shields her eyes. There's a click, and the guards unlock the cell door and enter 4C.

"What's going on?" Ilia asks.

"Mind your business, Halls. This isn't about you."

She recognizes the voice as her eyes adjust to the light. The guard who told her to clean up the body bag earlier stares, smiling. The other guard instructs them to stand against the wall then the first guard tears into the shared desk space and underneath the mattresses. He tosses trinkets and toilet paper across the floor.

"It's got to be here somewhere," he mumbles.

Ilia and Willow's eyes meet, but neither one seems to know what he's talking about. The women in the adjacent cells stir, and whispers of "shakedown" ripple through the air.

"Got it!" he finally exclaims.

He turns, and Ilia expects to see contraband—drugs or a knife or a cell phone that Willow hasn't told her about. Instead, he lifts up one of the books with the pages opened to the center and shows it to the other guard.

The necklace dangles, golden and thick, from his hand. Ilia feels her breath catch in her chest. "No, no, no," she whispers.

But he ignores her pleas and turns to Willow. "You think we wouldn't find this? You're coming with us. To the Hole."

She exchanges a pleading glance at Ilia then back at the guard. Her puckered mouth hardens. "Like hell I am," she says. "I don't know whose necklace that is or how it got in there, but—"

"But we do," the guard says. "And that's really all that matters. Restrain her."

They tackle Willow, and she kicks and screams and claws at every inch of flesh and fabric she can grab. Ilia presses against the wall, helpless as she watches them strike Willow over the head with a baton until she collapses. While she's unconscious, one of them cuffs her and throws her over the other guard's shoulder.

While he marches her limp body down the hall, the guard she knows lingers and locks their door again.

Ilia runs for the bars. "She didn't do anything. You *know* she didn't do anything," she insists.

"Now how would I know that, Halls? How would you?" He smiles again. "See you tomorrow, bright and early, for your next doc visit. That's more than your friend can say."

He glances over his shoulder as he struts down the row toward the Hole.

Sleep doesn't revisit Ilia. Overnight, she keeps glancing up at the bunk, expecting Willow's bare feet to be hanging there. By the time the guard appears again, she feels as if she's made another prison for herself, from worry and anger, inside the bars.

No words exchange between her and the guard. He cuffs her hands and walks her to the infirmary, to the same chair she succumbs to every time. It's a different nurse, just as she suspects, with the same blue caduceus neck tattoo. This woman doesn't even look at Ilia's face. She scribbles diligently in her thick file with its thick paperclip, then prepares the tourniquet, the needle, and the vials. Ilia's numb to the newness of the seat, the way she's buckled across her chest. Someone must have told this nurse about her history of passing out. She is relieved she doesn't need to explain it again.

Before the nurse can even tie a knot in the tourniquet, Ilia feels warmth, hears the high-pitched sting in her ears, and welcomes the gray-out.

She wakes pinned to the chair in the infirmary. The edges of everything around her resemble clouds. She blinks several times, trying to clear her vision, to little avail. Then she recognizes a figure in front of her—the backside of the nurse. She's talking to someone. Ilia thinks she hears the doctor's voice, but it sounds like he's far, far away.

She cocks her head and notices several dark figures hovering above like stringed balloons beside her. She squints, until the strings turn into tubes and the balloons into dozens of bags filled with dark red blood, suspended on hangers. She follows their red lines down to the fuzzy row of gurneys and women in jumpsuits beside her. She hears the incessant scream of one heart monitor gone flat, punctuated by all the rapid, beating hearts. Although the face is still murky, she can tell the woman next to her is crying.

"Let me out!" the muddied face shrieks at Ilia.

Ilia jumps but can't move. Straps hold her down. The voices and crying stop, and a tall, ghostly figure approaches. The doctor bends to the level of her eyes. "This one's ready for the Hole," his deep voice says.

"No," Ilia mouths. "What have you done to me?" Her lips feel numb and clumsy against her teeth. She isn't sure if her voice has left her throat, if the words moved from her brain to her lips. "Stop," she tries to say louder. She hears nothing but a long exhale and a gurgle. Her own gurgle.

"The eyes, doctor," the nurse says, ignoring her pleas. A fuzzy finger points at her skull. "Completely white in the center, like a cataract. Just as you advised."

"It never fails with these transfusions. That's your sign," the doctor says. *Transfusion?* Ilia wonders. "Let's ready her."

Ilia feels the nurse pull the needle and tape from her arm, then hears clicks to unbuckle the straps at her chest, wrists, and ankles. She feels herself slowly melting into the chair as the nurse calls a guard. Then she's lifted up by the arms. Her head falls forward, limp at the neck, and her shoes squeak along the linoleum.

"We meet again, Halls," the familiar, taunting voice of the guard whispers once they're alone. "Time to visit your friend."

The row is silent as he carries her past the cells, except for

Ilia's voice whispering "No, no, no" all the way to the Hole.

***

After Ilia sobers up and her eyes adjust to the blackness, she sees nothing. She slides her hands along the inner walls, trying to decipher the Hole's shape and depth. But it's irregular, with ill-placed concrete blocks jutting out from every surface.

She hears a moan behind her and turns, arms outstretched. "Willow?" she calls. But her voice is met with the silence of another cold wall. The moans return, muted from behind the wall. They come in waves for hours, maybe days. She wonders how long she can survive without food or water; if the moan is an old vent pushing air through, or is she still incapacitated, and the moan is imagined—or is it her own voice echoing off the walls. She wonders what new blood is pulsing in her veins and if she'll be cut into pieces and placed in a petri dish once it does whatever damage the doctor hopes for. She feels nothing different.

She wonders how long she's been getting transfusions. Since she was transferred? In the earlier prison as well? She curses her body for betraying her, for shutting down instead of fighting to stay awake, to watch. If she'd watched, she would have known something wasn't right.

She leans against the back wall and cries, softly at first, then echoing sobs. Then the wall behind her gives. She stumbles as a sliver of gray light spills onto the floor. At first Ilia thinks she's hallucinating, but as she presses her hand against the back wall, it swings open.

On the other side is a perfect mirror image of Block C. Dozens of empty cells sit underneath flickering florescent lights. The same smell of disinfectant and detergent and sweat all push against her. Yet it feels different.

The moan she keeps hearing rings from further down the row. She tip-toes out of the Hole toward the sound, past the empty cells to find other cells that are inhabited. No one whispers. No one stands, or reads books, or plays cards, or watches television. They all sit on their bunks, spiritless and still. Their heads are swollen, and their eyes are slits of puffy red flesh.

At the end of the corridor, a guard catches sight of Ilia and runs toward her. She freezes, and he grabs her by the arms. She's pulled toward a cell, 4C.

The same but not, she thinks.

"Patient Halls acquired," the guard says into his radio. "Dropping her off at her cell. Copy. Over." Static muffles the reply. "Didn't think you'd get away so easily, did you?" he says. He shoves her inside.

A shiver runs up her spine as she stares at a figure in the cell with her. A lump of a human being sits on the bottom bunk, with hands covering its face, skin so swollen it could burst.

The bars slam shut, and the guard wanders off, still chit-chatting code into his radio.

"I knew you'd come eventually," the inmate groans.

Ilia's lower lip begins to quiver when she recognizes the voice. "Willow?"

Willow stares up at Ilia with milk-white eyes and a marred expression. Instead of a fully swollen face like the others, half of her body, head to toe, is puffy and distended. A growth snakes around her neck like an inner tube. Along her swollen lips, Ilia notices the scab.

"Willow?" she repeats. Then the words vomit out of her in short gasps. "Oh my God. Oh my God. No, no, no ... What did they do to you?" she screams. Sobs overtake Ilia's body, and she begs, helplessly, "Why?" until she exhausts herself and falls to her knees beside the bunk.

She reaches out to hold Willow's swollen hand, but Willow retreats, afraid to be touched. This only makes Ilia cry harder and louder, until her throat goes raw.

When Ilia can't cough up another sob, Willow speaks. "They told me the treatments were to help my depression, Ilia," she says, "to help me get better, so I could get out of here. But it was all a lie. This is a lab, and we're the rats. The warden has a deal with the doctor, and that's why everyone who goes to the Hole doesn't come out again."

"But why us?"

"Think about it. We're both already sick, and we've got life sentences. At this point, no one in the system cares if we disappear."

Ilia wipes her eyes. "Who told you all of this? One of the nurses who keep disappearing?"

"No, I think the nurses—if they're even real nurses—are paid hush money. They don't stay long. As for the rest, I overheard the doctor and warden talking outside of the Hole when they took me away. The warden pocketed money. He said this, meaning you and me, were it for the month or people on the outside would start asking questions. It's more hopeless than I thought, Ilia."

Willow starts to sob now. Half of her at least. The other half jiggles with each gasp for air. As she moves, Ilia notices a spot of ink above her collar. She pulls back the fabric to find the caduceus along Willow's bloated neck, just like the woman in the body bag.

"God almighty," she whispers as she realizes the body with

the necklace could have been any woman who was part of the prison experiments.

"You've got one now, too. I guarantee it," Willow says. "They probably did it while you were passed out."

Ilia grasps her own neck and feels the mild swelling, the itch of dry skin. She can't see it, but she knows Willow's right. She knows the caduceus is branded on her, too.

"How long until it happens? To me?" she clarifies. "And then what?"

Willow turns toward her. "Then nothing. They realize they haven't found a cure—again—and you're left to die. They'll give you food, sure, but the swelling gets so bad you can't eat it. Either your skin cracks open, like an explosion in slow-motion, or you strangle yourself with your own neck." Ilia shudders as Willow stretches over the bottom bunk. "If it's alright by you, I want to stay on the bottom bunk. It hurts too bad to climb to the top, and you can see better than I can for now. When you start to swell, too, we can take turns or both sleep down here."

"Sure," Ilia says softly. She climbs to the top bunk, even though part of her wants to rest beside Willow, to never let her out of her sight again, even if it means finding her in a puddle of flesh tomorrow morning.

"Ilia?" Willow squeaks. "You didn't bring a book with you, did you?"

"I wish," she replies.

"You remember anything? Or can you make something up?"

Ilia feels like she's cracking from the inside but isn't sure if it's from the transfusion or hopelessness or both. But she begins reciting her favorite passage from *Their Eyes Were Watching God*. It isn't long until the cell is overtaken by Willow's gentle snores.

Ilia fingers the tattoo along her neck, feeling the tissue puckered and rising like bread. She wonders how long it will be until it overtakes her. She wonders if it will be a quick death.

Nothing happens for days, though. Ilia's eyes don't morph into fissures. Her neck doesn't balloon. When she examines her arms every few minutes, even if it's just a glance or a pinch, everything seems normal.

Willow's swelling gradually pours into both sides of her body then bubbles up to her head and neck, just like the others. Sometimes it's hard for her to get out of bed or sit upright because, as she says, it feels like she's carrying a bowling ball on her shoulders.

Ilia feels them watching wherever she goes. The guards with their stern inspection of her. The other inmates, their tiny pupils crying out for help behind slits of inflamed flesh. *Why you and not me?* those eyes seem to say. She knows they all question why she's not transforming into a monster. She does, too.

So she isn't surprised when two guards cuff her and lead her to the infirmary on this side of the Hole. Willow tries to place her body in between the guards and Ilia, but she topples over onto the floor just trying to stand.

When Ilia sees the doctor and nurse from the transfusion earlier, she scowls. Their faces are half-covered with masks, as if they're afraid she's contagious, even though she's the only inmate without symptoms.

"Have a seat," the doctor says in his muffled voice.

She refuses, but the guards force her down and restrain her with straps across her chest.

"Call us when she's done," they say. Then they march off to other duties.

Both the doctor and nurse turn toward Ilia again. "We need to figure out why you're not mutating," the doctor says. "Do you have any medical conditions that weren't previously disclosed? Allergies? Any new symptoms that have appeared since the treatment?"

Ilia refuses to answer.

"Have you been making or taking any illegal substances? Pills somebody on the outside slipped you?"

Ilia sneers. "You know we're not allowed to have visitors," she says through gritted teeth.

"Maybe something your cell mate gave you, like an antidote, since she knew what would happen?"

Ilia feels blood race into her earlobes. "You leave her out of this. You've already done enough to her, to all of them. We didn't deserve this."

The doctor shakes his head at the floor and chuckles. "When we don't have answers, Ilia—when you aren't honest with us—we can only lean on science. And good science says we evaluate a hypothesis. Here's the theory: your most recent transfusion was flawed in some way. Error is actually quite common in experiments. The goal, though, is to find errors before they affect the results. So if we transfuse you again, my guess is you'll have a reaction just like the other test subjects did."

She shudders but keeps her voice steady. "I said no. I mean it."

"I'm not asking. You have no choice. If you survive a second transfusion, then America's newest biochemical weapon needs tweaking, and I'd be doing a disservice to the handful of politicians sponsoring our lab if I didn't go back to the drawing board. But if you don't survive, then we've found the error and squashed it. Either way, science wins."

Ilia's mind races.

He motions over the nurse. "Prepare the patient while I wash up, please." He exits through the swinging door.

The nurse cradles a syringe. "I know you usually pass out, but this is a safer way to get you to sleep—and stay asleep. Everything needs to go perfectly this time."

Ilia feels perspiration break out across her brow. The voice inside her head starts again. *Don't resort to violence!* But she shoves it down. Her eyes dart between the syringe and the door. The nurse flicks the side of the syringe as clear droplets spill from the tip, bends over, and rolls up Ilia's sleeve. She pinches the flesh.

Ilia eyes the tattoo along the nurse's neck, then her gaze travels up to the nurse's temple. She jerks her head forward. Their skulls crack against each other, and the nurse grasps the arm of the Ilia's chair. The syringe falls into Ilia's lap. She grabs it with her cuffed hands and kicks the nurse's shins. The nurse collapses onto Ilia's lap and glances up, disoriented. Ilia jams the needle right in the middle of the caduceus and injects the fluid. The nurse slumps onto the floor.

For a few moments, Ilia tries to calm her breathing, then she remembers the doctor. She pushes her chest against the restraint until she's red in the face, but it stretches just enough for her to slip out from underneath.

She listens for the doctor's footsteps but hears nothing. Frantically, she searches the room for something to free her from the cuffs. Once, when her husband was away at work, she attended a free self-defense clinic at the Y. They showed her how to use a bobby pin to break into a pair of cuffs, but they aren't allowed to have bobby pins or clips of any kind at the prison.

"Clips!" she whispers. She races over to her file on the countertop and the fat, black binder clip that pinches the papers together. Her hands and teeth pull and twist to release one of the metal pieces, then she forces the tip through the keyhole, trying to release the lock. But it doesn't budge.

Shit, a double lock. She scrambles as footsteps approach from the hall, twisting in one direction until the side pin recedes, then twisting it quickly the other direction until she's free.

The door creaks open. She hides behind it, holding her breath. She hears the doctor's footsteps pause, and he bends down to turn the nurse onto her back.

Ilia reaches a hand toward the countertop and grabs the tourniquet. As he curses and raises the empty syringe toward the fluorescent lights, she leaps out from behind the door and wraps the tourniquet around his neck. He thrashes, but she keeps her grip, riding him like a wild animal until he's convulsing on the floor. She squeezes tighter for good measure, until his body relaxes. He lies motionless beneath her.

Ilia bends down and undresses the nurse. She slips into the uniform and face mask and grabs the badge and keys that have fallen onto the floor. Just outside the door, she sees an empty body bag on a gurney. She zips it up and rolls forward, keeping her head down.

"Good evening," a guard in the hallway says. She says nothing but nods and grips the gurney as she pushes past him toward Block C.

When she reaches 4C she halts the gurney and fumbles with the keys, trying to find one to release the lock.

"It's me," Ilia hisses. "Get up. We don't have much time." The lock pops open and she pushes the gurney beside the bunks.

"Get in."

"Why are you dressed like a nurse? Is this for Halloween? They actually let you do that?"

"Shh," she whispers. "Keep your voice down! I sedated the nurse and strangled the doctor. But we don't have much time to get out of here before they realize what I've done. I want you to crawl inside this body bag and pretend to be dead."

Willow shakes her head in disbelief. "I don't have to pretend. You're going to get us killed."

Desperation creeps into Ilia's voice. "We're already dead, remember, Willow? We've been dead since the word 'guilty.' It's now or never."

Willow sighs and crawls onto the gurney, bracing her swollen head with both hands, and Ilia helps her lie flat and zips the top closed.

"Don't ask me anything. Don't say anything, from here on out. I don't care if I scream for help. You stay put. Got it?"

Willow says nothing.

"Good job," Ilia replies.

Ilia slides the prison door open and glances in both directions, searching for anyone who may be searching for them. When she realizes it's just them, she pushes down the row and out into other hallways, meandering, trying to find a way to leave. But the prison seems to circle back into itself.

"What's going on?" Willow moans.

"Shh. We're not in the clear yet."

She rounds a corner and sees an exit sign through a set of doors, past the infirmary. Ilia swipes her badge and starts rolling in that direction when she hears "Hey! Halls!" from behind them.

She stalls, uncertain if she should bolt for the exit or turn around. Hoping to avoid suspicion, she turns around. The bodies of the doctor and nurse can still be seen on the floor where she left them. She holds her breath.

"Hey! Is that Halls? The patient I just took for transfusion earlier?" It's the menacing guard. He's so close she can smell his breath again. He stops just steps shy of view into the medical room.

Ilia hesitates then mutters, "I believe that's what the file said."

The guard's frown turns into a smile, and he starts snickering. "Good riddance. It's too easy with these freaks."

Ilia slowly nods her head.

He waves her on with his hand, as if he's instructing her to take out the trash and turns, disappearing down the hall.

She shuffles forward then bolts for the door. When no alarms sound at the exit, she runs faster, the gurney bouncing side to side along the gravel, until they're past the parking lot under the guise of night. She reaches the end of a long drive that collides with the main road, an abandoned road, where all Ilia can see is stars. Behind a screen of nearby trees, she unzips the body bag and helps Willow climb out.

They trudge, hand in hand, through a grassy field, with Ilia leading the way. The closest lights along the horizon are small, what feels like too many miles away. But Ilia knows it's a neighborhood. She can feel it. Ilia hears the whistle of a train, but not just in her head this time. Out there. Headed toward the patch of light.

"Let's go," Ilia says, pulling harder on Willow. "We'll find a hospital. We'll find your children. We'll make those motherfuckers pay."

But Willow's frozen. "I—I can't," she starts. "You heard

him. We're nothing but freaks, especially out here." She gasps for air, as if she's about to cry, but no tears are able to squeeze through the tight flesh of her face. "What if my children don't recognize me? What if they scream and run away? They will. You know they will. Don't lie to me. Look at me!"

Ilia's jaw is agape.

"It's been too long, Ilia. I don't know how to live out there. I was never good at it anyway. Just put me back in the body bag, please! Please! I'm going to end up there anyway!"

She tries to climb onto the gurney, only to push it farther away and stumbles into the grass. Laughter and shouts of "Trick-or-treat!" rise like ghosts in the direction of the train then disappear as they roll by in the autumn wind.

Ilia bends down and brushes her fingertips along Willow's back until her sobs subside. Then she helps Willow to her feet and pulls her toward the sounds and the light.

"How did your dream end, Willow? The one where we were out here, on Halloween? But I wasn't me, and you weren't you?"

"We were together," Willow says. "That's all I remember."

Acknowledgments

Thank you to everyone who took the time to read my early drafts and respond with honest feedback, who kept asking for more stories, and who purchased publications where my stories were featured. Thank you to *New Gothic Review*, Jolly Horror Press, Scare Street, and *Coffin Bell* journal for taking a chance on some of my earlier work. I'm still honored you saw something special there.

An extra special thank you to Wendy Dalrymple (author of *Roser Park* and *White Ibis*) for her friendship, mentorship, indie author advice, inside scoop on new open calls for fiction, the Forward, the kick-ass tagline for this collection . . . the list goes on.

I would also like to thank my mother, Annette, who is always my first reader, and my husband, Jim, who is always willing to be the mirror for my weird and shapeless story ideas in their infancy.

Thank you as well to Patty of Seeing Eye Editing for her discerning eye and to Tea Jagodic for the riveting cover.

About the Author

Jenna Dietzer is a technology process geek by day and writer by night. She lives in Tampa, Florida with her husband and their fur-kids. When she's not writing, you'll find her chasing down Florida folklore on local ghost tours, decorating way too early for Halloween, or watching documentaries about—what else?—murder. Her work has been featured in the Executive Dread anthology by Jolly Horror Press, Scare Street Night Terrors Vol. 21, Coffin Bell, and New Gothic Review. *Fear Her* is her debut short story collection.

You can connect with me on:
- https://twitter.com/duh_jenna
- https://www.facebook.com/JennaDietzerAuthor
- https://www.instagram.com/jenna.dietzer